Strange Sands Suspense 2
Savannah

The Hidden Hallway

Pamela Poole

Southern Sky Publishing

I0544217

Cover picture is created using Craiyon tools
Cover created on BookBrush
Ebook ISBN: 9781956089172
Print ISBN: 9781956089189
Print ISBN: 9781956089196

Author's Note

Have you ever walked into a place and instantly became ill at ease? Did you ever meet a person and your spirit clashed with his or hers? Was there ever a time when you couldn't explain it, but you simply knew something bad might happen at any moment—and it did?

The novellas in the Strange Sands Suspense series will follow the adventures of a young lady named Mercedes Ellison, whose family has a long history of unexplainable encounters that many would call "strange." But then, Christians are peculiar people who should be living supernatural lives.

The stories and people in this series are fictional, but they are steeped in places I've been, situations I've experienced, and people I interviewed who have had a few of these encounters—encounters they typically keep to themselves. Each story contains at least one of the events from my interviews.

I hope you'll enjoy the Southern Lowcountry ambiance in this series, where moments spent on warm sandy beaches blend with the grains of slipping sand in history's hourglass.

Chapter 1

If we understand that everything happening to us is to make us more Christlike, it will solve a great deal of anxiety in our lives.
A.W. Tozer, in *The Crucified Life*

"Oh, no," Mercedes said out loud to herself. Arriving at a crime scene was no way to meet a new client—dead or alive.

She sighed and drove past the police cars at the historic property in Savannah, Georgia, where she had an appointment with Tammy and Clayton Popplewell, a couple who fled big city life in the northern United States. They purchased a run-down historic house to restore, hoping to rent rooms or open an inn. The site was a good one for their plans, within walking distance of some of the beautiful park squares in Savannah, but it needed a lot of work.

There was street parking a block away. Mercedes pulled over, leaving the air conditioning on as she picked up her phone to text Tammy Popplewell. While she waited for a response, she sent a text to Quincy Holmwood.

Tammy Popplewell sent back a text to tell her to come on in for their appointment. Her husband was with the police in the backyard and would finish soon.

Quincy sent a text that made her laugh. *Ellisons don't show up at ruined houses and expect a job anyone else can do. When you finish the exorcism, want to have lunch with me back here in little ole Bluffton? I can take a break at noon. We'll eat in broad daylight and order something with garlic. I'll bring our pure silver utensils.*

Still smiling, she answered. *Love to. I'll let you know if I can be back up there during your lunch break.* She checked her visor mirror to put on a light natural color of lip balm. Then she smoothed her breezy summer blouse before turning off the engine, gathered her purse and digital tablet, and opened her door to the oppressive humidity that promised a coming thunderstorm.

As she followed a sidewalk veined with the roots of elderly magnolia trees, Mercedes noted the various styles of architecture on the same street as her new clients. They had a Federal architectural style house as one side neighbor and a loose Georgian style on the other. But the front facade of this house was firmly Creole Townhouse style, with strong Spanish and Caribbean influences. The Creole style was popular from about 1788 through mid-eighteen hundred and this house loosely dated in the Antebellum era as pre-Civil War. The style would have been common in New Orleans but was unusual in Savannah, and that was the reason she was excited about working with the Popplewell couple to restore it.

She stopped to admire the front of the house, which stood with dignity like a Southern belle in a black lace shawl. A shabby brick walkway, step-up porch, and three brick-lined steps provided the setting for once-beautiful double front doors. Lacy iron scrollwork protected leaded paned glass on the upper half of the door. It was the same style that graced the front of the house, running up corners of the porch, along the eaves, and into a fence from the porch to the side of the house. A walkway led to an ornately arched gate of the same ironwork.

The facade of the second floor of the house imitated the porch under it, duplicating the scrolling black iron. Faded yellow siding still created a cheerful impression overall, and she decided it was an unusual house with plenty of personality.

Tammy Popplewell opened the front door and stepped out. "You must be Mercedes Ellison. You look just like the photo on your website. I'm Tammy!"

Mercedes went to the porch and smiled back at her client. "Yes, I'm Mercedes. I'm excited to meet you, Tammy. I was just thinking how much personality this property has."

Her client's eyes clouded with trouble. "Yes, it has that. Come on inside, Mercedes. My husband will be free in a few minutes."

The entrance hall through the double front doors had been impressive at one time. The musty odor of decay and neglect greeted Mercedes now, however, and garish large flora on peeling wallpaper was evidence of a lapse in good taste by a previous owner. Nearby, the ruins of an armchair in the same colors backed against the wall, and overhead, broken strings of grimy crystals hung from a chandelier.

Three police officers came through the hall into the once-grand entryway with Tammy's husband, Clayton, and there were introductions all around. The officers were courteous and silent while Clayton told Mercedes they had an adventure early that morning, but there was no reason not to proceed with their meeting and plans.

Mercedes felt one of the young officers studying her and met his eyes. He half-smiled and nodded politely. She looked over at Clayton and asked, "Will I have access to the police report? It could have implications for my paperwork."

The Popplewell couple both agreed, and Clayton saw the officers out the front doors. Tammy still wore the troubled look Mercedes noticed when they met. "Tammy, your mind's not on the things we need to cover today. Will it help to talk about what happened?"

Clayton came back in, and Tammy said, "Let's tell Mercedes about the intruder, and you should tell me what the police said. I can't focus on our appointment with Mercedes until we talk this through."

He sighed and came to hug her, then he turned to Mercedes. "Let's go into the kitchen for tea and coffee. There's an air conditioner back there. Tammy and I cleaned up the kitchen, a bedroom, and a bathroom to use for ourselves while we plan for restoration and remodeling."

Mercedes sat at a painted vintage kitchen table with her newest clients. It was small, and the chipped paint revealed its past lives in several colors, but someone had scrubbed it clean. She sipped herbal tea while Tammy Popplewell announced, "I'm not staying here tonight."

In a patient tone, Clayton said, "I understand how you feel, but we agreed to stay on site until we get a schedule and work can begin. We aren't even certain any crime occurred."

"I locked that door, Clayton, and the footprints aren't my imagination."

Mercedes kept her voice gentle. "Tammy, tell me your version of what happened."

"Before dawn, I woke up feeling like something was wrong. It was damp in the house and the air was stirring, but not from our little air conditioner unit. Then I saw the bedroom door was open. Sure, Clayton might have gotten up to use the bathroom and forgot to close it, but when I saw it, my heart jumped. There was something sinister about it. I was on the side of the bed closest to the black hole in the open door. I shook Clayton to wake him, and he said he closed the door because of the room air conditioner and the musty smell of the house. We got up to look around, and the back door stood open. There had been rain after we went to bed, and footprints were in the crushed, wet grass. Not definable enough to say what kind of shoes the intruder wore, though."

"If the intruder came in through the door, he removed his shoes or cleaned up any trace of wet tracks that would give him away," said Clayton. "We really don't know what to make of it, but the open door of the bedroom really spooked Tammy." He reached over and rubbed his wife's hand.

"May I see the outdoor footprints?" asked Mercedes.

The couple took her out to the backyard, and Mercedes followed the bruised grass and slight impressions of a person's weight in the sandy soil to an outdoor building. There was a crusty nail and the ghostly outline of a key shape on the rotting wood wall near where the foot tracks ended, but no key dangled there now. "This looks like it was once a servant's quarters, or a guest house. Is it used for storage?"

"I haven't been inside it. It's locked, and they boarded the windows up. The real estate agent said they marked the building to be demolished, and we understood they would do it before we arrived, so I doubt we have a claim on whatever is inside. I'll call her about it today."

Mercedes scanned the area for more tracks. "Where do the police think the intruder entered and exited the backyard?"

Clayton pointed to a wooden privacy screen. "The yard has a low iron fence behind the overgrowth along the sides, but behind that raggedy hedge at the back of the property is an old wood screen with a ramshackle gate in it. It's rickety and the rusty hinges grind, but someone could open it and stoop under the shrubbery."

She and Tammy followed him to the hedge, where they could barely make out the top of the warped and weathered wooden fence. Along the way, they found more bruised grass and a dirt footpath under some bottle-brush bushes that bristled with red blooms.

Mercedes studied the evidence of uninvited guests on the Popplewell property. "The house has been sitting empty a long time, and kids might have been hanging out around it. Did the police visit the homeowners behind you to learn whether they saw anything unusual?"

"They were going there next and said they would update me if they learned anything. There are occasional calls about teenagers lurking around, but they have committed no crimes other than trespassing. The complaints increase in the summer when schools are out. The officers think kids might believe the house is still empty, but it doesn't account for where the back door key is. I'll change that lock today, and I'll put one on that gate, too. Looks like we'll be making a trip to the hardware store."

They walked back toward the house, and Mercedes paused again at the dilapidated outbuilding. "I suspect there was once a key hanging on that nail and it might have been for the back door. Various occupants of the house probably thought it was a safe place to keep a spare if they locked themselves out. A thief is more likely to look under the welcome mat or a flowerpot than a nail on an outbuilding."

She searched her tablet for records on the property. "It appears the original owners of the house had no slaves but had servants, and this was quarters for a gardener. You hired me for all the boring work, specifics about the historic guidelines and the paperwork that is required for restoration. But if I see any other records and correspondence relating to previous owners, I'll be glad to investigate any valid accounts about the history of the property."

Tammy said, "Yes, please check into the history of this house. All we know about it is what the real estate records report—the year they think someone built it, ownership changes, that sort of thing. The agent did mention that the houses on this street survived the fire of 1898 because they had tin roofs, which resisted the embers from other structures. This is the original building, except for remodeling over the years."

Mercedes noticed Clayton studying her, so she asked, "Is further investigation to dig up history on the house okay with you? It shouldn't take much time, but if it does, I will have to charge for an extra hour or two."

"Yes, having the history will add value to our investment in the house, and it might direct some of our decorating choices. But I find it curious that you seem focused on this building, and you think there's a story about it in the property's history."

Taken aback, Mercedes raised her brows. She looked at the building again, studying it. "Yes, I came straight here, didn't I? I suppose I followed the footprints. Someone else who was in your yard after last night's rain had an interest in the building. So, it piques my curiosity."

Tammy took her arm. "Come on, look at that bedroom doorway."

"We hired a cleaning crew to get everything in this place cleared out," Clayton said as they left the kitchen through a door that opened to a living room and hallway. "They planned to finish yesterday, which is why we timed things to sleep here last night. It would have smelled better in here. But they called with an emergency and rescheduled for tomorrow."

His phone rang, and he asked Tammy to continue showing Mercedes around while he talked to the real estate agent about the building out back. He went outside while Tammy led Mercedes to the living room and entryway.

Mercedes winced as she glanced around the room and saw a tarnished, brassy, fat-bellied statue of an idol and an unboxed seance game. A deck of worn-out tarot cards, crystals, an eye symbol, and a pyramid sat on top of a stack of old books on magic and witchcraft. Grotesque half-animal carvings on incense burners rested in thick dust near a tiny golden shrine in a corner and nearby were candle stubs and a box of matches. In a window hung a dreamcatcher draped in spider webs, and on the crumbling plaster wall, a dusty, faded tapestry with pagan worship scenes in mythology was hanging by two nails, one corner dangling.

"Tammy, I need to snap photos of the house with my tablet camera," said Mercedes. "But there are occult objects scattered around in this room, and I don't want them in my device, even as images. I'm not putting them in the permanent records of this property, so I'll return after they clean the house. Personally, I support your conviction not to stay here tonight. Absolutely do not."

"Occult objects?" asked Tammy, with a blank expression.

Mercedes shifted her weight to one foot and hugged her tablet to her waist, praying for words that would not make her sound crazy. "Since you told me you're a Christian, I hope you'll understand if I seem eccentric. Many people don't realize how mainstream occult images have become, as trends in home décor, collectibles, exercise, games, and jewelry. But they represent symbolism linked to cults and idols, and I try to avoid them. The Bible isn't clear whether an evil entity can inhabit objects, but it inspired them, and can carry a level of authority. Meaning, I believe if we collect them or keep them close to us, like in our décor or things we wear and read, we have given them a right to be there. In my own life, I try to apply Paul's teaching in 1 Corinthians 10:20-22 about not taking part with demons."

Unaware of their conversation, Clayton walked back inside and launched into telling them about his phone call. "The agent tells me she and the former property management agency are talking to another company about the demolition. The one they hired first has either gone bankrupt or had to leave town for unpaid debts. So, I don't have a date yet about getting rid of the building. The agent also told me there is another key to the back door, and it was missing when we closed on the house. Our mystery intruder may have had it and thought the place was empty. Maybe we frightened him as much as he frightened us."

Tammy still wore a blank look, as if she had too much information to process at once, so Mercedes asked for the tour of the house to continue. Clayton took over, and he chattered about their challenges to make a portion of the house livable. He led Mercedes past the staircase to a gloomy hallway leading to the room he and his wife had as a temporary bedroom. When he opened the door, cool air greeted them, and the musty smell of the old house improved with the added aroma of magnolias in bloom. The wooden paneled door was taller than an average one, suiting the tall ceilings, and it wore generations of paint layers that peeled in places. Otherwise, it was ordinary. Still, when she let her imagination picture it wide open to the black hallway at night, she felt a chill.

Dimly lit, depressing hallways with the rectangular ghosts of former portraits on the walls led to many rooms in the house, and with the addition of planned bathrooms, she could see why the Popplewells hoped to transform it into an inn or boarding house. But some walls were confusing. They didn't work out right in her mind, according to space and symmetry.

She walked past a wall at the split staircase that was out of place architecturally. The railing did not match and there was an odd, ugly cutout section to a hall on the first floor from the landing. Then she walked back into a room with a door to another room, which should have had separate doors, like the downstairs version. The rooms were too small to account for the area by the staircase, and there was no closet.

Mercedes scowled at the page on her tablet, puzzled. "If you don't mind, will you let me know when your contractor is coming to evaluate the layout of the house and give you some estimates? According to my records of the house and from looking at the rooms, there is space that's unaccounted for."

Tammy and Clayton looked at each other in surprise. Clayton's voice was eager when he asked, "You mean, like, hidden rooms and passages?"

Mercedes smiled. "It's a romantic notion, but anything's possible. People used to live when it was important to hide belongings, have an escape route, or maybe just cover up a drafty old fireplace."

With a sparkle in his eyes, Clayton said, "We will call when the contractor gives us a date and time."

Mercedes ran a few minutes later to get from Savannah to Bluffton for her lunch date with Quincy. She called him from the sidewalk as she left the Popplewell's house, asking him to order for her if he was tight on his window of time. He said he was running late, too, and would reschedule a meeting that afternoon so they could relax. "After all, we live in Lowcountry time," he drawled, abandoning his slightly British accent to imitate the Southern voices he heard everywhere now.

As she walked from her parking spot toward the restaurant, Quincy was getting out of a sparkling Mercedes convertible, top down. His suntan, sporty sunglasses, and resort casual attire brought out all his best features. The sight made her catch her breath and squash a gush of emotion. Then he noticed her and grinned, looking both ways and jogging across the street.

"Really, Quincy? A *Mercedes*?" she squeaked.

He laughed and winked, then took her arm to go to the door. "Sure! It's the only way I'll ever control a Mercedes. It appeals to my dreams. Like it?"

"It beats the anonymous white sedan," she smirked. "I'm just so used to seeing you in a dust and mud-spattered Hummer, Jeep or Land Rover in the middle of nowhere anyone wants to be." Then she sighed and grinned. "Okay, yes, I love your car. It's gorgeous and you look very handsome in it. Expect a lot of attention from other wishful thinkers, many of them women."

He was laughing at her when a young host asked whether they preferred indoor or outdoor seating. Mercedes quickly told him she wanted to be indoors. "I've spent a lot of time in a humid house with no air conditioning today," she explained to Quincy, who was pushing his sunglasses up on his head. "Not to mention that it smelled like ruin and decay, and I probably carry the odor on me now. But at least there was no sign of rancid animal filth on the floors, probably because of a no pet policy for the renters who lived there over the years."

"Did you explain to the owners that you can't work closely inside houses that have had animals in them?"

"Yes, it's in the paperwork in the initial interviews to screen clients."

A server brought out frosty water glasses and nautical-themed menus, and they focused on their lunch orders. Both chose a hearty salad topped with blackened grouper. They declined a basket of bread and hushpuppies but ordered rosemary potato fries to share.

Quincy reached for Mercedes' hand across the table and prayed thanks over the meal, and her heart leaped when he thanked the Lord for the blessing of having her to join him. Then they enjoyed their lunch and conversation. The noon rush in the seafood-themed restaurant was over, leaving a relaxed atmosphere of diners who were living in Lowcountry time with no place to rush off to, even if they wanted to leave.

"Um, this is so good," commented Quincy between bites. "The food, the river, the beaches and parks—I was crazy to think it would be hard to settle down in one place. I'm honestly glad the insanity of the world forced me to decide about my priorities and what I'm going to do the rest of my life."

Mercedes kept her eyes on her salad and finished another bite while considering her response. "You had a lot of experiences over the years, living in rough conditions in the field. Which was your favorite?"

He swallowed iced tea and took a deep breath. "Anywhere you were. Those were my favorites."

She bit her lip. "We made some of my fondest memories, too. I still dream about those times now and then. What about going home?"

"Oh, sure, it was nice to see my grandparents and my parents if they weren't on the same site I was working. But the entire family will eventually move here. Keeping up the estate took a ridiculous amount of money and there's no way to justify it for good stewardship."

Mercedes set her water glass down and glanced around the décor of the restaurant. "What about your friends and relationships there?"

He sat straight in his chair, stretching his shoulders, and clearing his throat. "I can see you didn't keep up with me through our parents. My friends that remain in England still communicate as if I'm traveling, and most were from around the world anyway, you know that. If by relationships you mean romantic entanglements, I went out occasionally when I was home. Some friend of the family always had a daughter or niece who needed an escort. Those aren't hard to leave behind. As for the one I got involved with for revenge when you said we had no future together because of our goals, she lasted about six weeks, while you moved on to enjoy a year with Zach."

"Can I get you anything? Dessert?" The server stood by their table with a bright smile. She swiftly removed their empty dishes and enticed them with a memorized list of delicious sweets.

Mercedes smiled back and shook her head, saying the meal was wonderful and she ate too much. Quincy agreed and told the server it was okay to bring the check. Then he leaned his elbows on the lacquered wood tabletop and looked intently at Mercedes.

"I quickly regretted the revenge relationship. She was less than an inch deep and nothing like you, as you already knew. That stunt was beneath me and while my goal of hurting you probably worked, it drove you to your instant attachment to a long-distance romance with Zach. I'm sorry. I didn't know how to deal with losing you and giving up my dreams, but my goals changed rapidly, pulled out from under me, really. It was unreal and unsettling, but it was for the best. When you get over Zach, can we talk about picking up where we left off, adjusting to the people we've become?"

Mercedes glanced away, composing her thoughts. Picking up where they left off was just shy of an engagement ring. It was unclear how much either of them changed, and adjustments sounded risky, but there was room for hope.

She looked back at him. "Are you sure you won't feel tied down?"

The waitress brought a little folder with the bill for lunch in it, and Quincy reached for his wallet. He put cash into the folder and left it on the edge of the table. Then he reached across for Mercedes' hand, and she put hers in it.

"I won't feel tied down," he replied solemnly. "My heart and mind changed before the world altered so drastically. It wasn't hard to give up, Mercedes. I just wasn't ready when you asked. If your timing had been a couple of months later, we never would have broken up. I'm an idiot."

She bit her lower lip and blinked, looking down when the server came and asked if Quincy wanted any change back. He said no, and she gushed her thanks and wished them a fantastic day.

Mercedes' hand was still in his while he waited for an answer. She composed herself, then she met his eyes again. "There's nothing for me to get over with Zach, except maybe some anger. I couldn't get past losing you and being rejected for the career you dreamed of. Being with him was a step toward accepting the way things were and making a life without you in it, and I ended that experiment the night I went down to Hilton Head."

He sighed and squeezed her hand. "Is there anything about the past year that we need to hash out? Any hard feelings?"

"No. I honestly wanted you to be a star in the world of archaeology and antiquities, and I knew I was only in your way. I didn't talk about you with my parents or yours because it would hurt to hear about the love in your life. But I followed your blog and website videos when you were being brilliant on site somewhere. You mentioned no romantic entanglements, so it was safe to see what you were working on. You didn't do one about changing your role and coming to live here."

"Right, I haven't updated in a while. I became overwhelmed with the logistics of quitting and settling back here in the States, as well as jumping on board with the investigation of Lenoir as we closed in on him. I lost my enthusiasm—everything I did, everything my family ever accomplished for history, it all seems meaningless. Maybe you can help me get things started again."

Now, she was the one who squeezed his hand. "I don't know if I can live up to all that, Quincy, but if you've truly reconsidered the future, I want a second chance to be together."

I saw this house in Savannah in 2010 and fell in love with it! Afterwards, I created this painting of it in my studio, and writing this novel gave me a reason to put it into a story. The Popplewell house is double this one in size, with the doors being the center and more windows on the side where the gate is.

-Pamela Poole

Chapter 2

Mercedes spent the afternoon in her cottage, completing another round of paperwork for the job she was still finishing in Bluffton and researching the history of the Popplewell's house. In late afternoon, she got a text from Tammy, thanking her for coming by and saying that though she had some reservations about the house after what happened with the intruder, she and Clayton were moving forward with their plans and looking forward to working with her.

Tammy told her husband about being sure the cleaning crew disposed of the offending décor and items left by a previous tenant in the house tomorrow. She wrote, *He thought you were over the top about it and was going to prove it to me by looking up the things on the internet. He was shocked and had to admit you knew what you were talking about. Clayton gave in to my intuition about not sleeping here tonight. We'll be staying in a hotel room for a couple of nights while the house gets cleaned.*

With a sigh, Mercedes texted back. *I'm glad you made other arrangements for now. If Clayton thinks I'm eccentric, tell him I'm used to it, and he has a lot of company. Did he get new locks on the gate and back door?*

Yes. He wanted to have a look in the outbuilding but can't budge the lock.

Tammy, please tell him not to do that unless the contractor is there! The building isn't safe, or they would not slate it for demolition. I'm working on your paperwork and learning some history about the house right now. Has the contractor made an appointment yet?

The next text said, *I told Clayton you wouldn't like him nosing around like that! He still underestimates you because you're young and pretty. Yes, the contractor will be here the day after tomorrow. The house should get cleared out and empty then, except for the kitchen and the bedroom Clayton and I are using.*

Mercedes looked at her calendar and jotted down a note. *Okay, text me a time when he expects to be there. I won't schedule anything else that day until I hear from you. Did the police reach out to Clayton after talking to the back yard neighbors?*

Tammy texted back. *Oh, I almost forgot to update you about that! Yes, they did. I'll fill you in when I see you. Also, one officer asked Clayton for your name and why you were here. He told them we were working with you, so the house gets registered correctly with the historical places agencies and that you were helping steer us in the right direction for restorations.*

One officer was curious about her that morning, Mercedes knew. Did he know something about the recent news at the beach house on Hilton Head? Her name, and the other attendees' names, were to be kept out of the media. Until her attackers faced their day in court, she was to be given privacy so she could live and work in peace.

Well, the officer should accept Clayton's answer, unless I become a suspect or a nuisance, she texted, and added a winking emoticon.

The text from Tammy was a line of laughing emoticons.

After eating a light dinner in the cottage, Mercedes met Quincy in the driveway to take Bijou for a walk around the block. She still laughed every time she saw a tall, rugged

Quincy with the silly and adorable miniature designer dog. Today's leash color was magenta, and the sequins covering it shimmered in the late light of the day. The dog's owner was recovering from a sprained ankle and could manage a short walk now, but Bijou sat at the storm door glass, looking for Quincy.

"I'll let her ease her way back into being walked by her mommy. I'm taking the evening shift," he said. "But soon, I'll be all yours. I'm loving swimming in Lois' pool every night."

"So, Bijou is my only competition to having you all to myself?" she teased, accepting his elbow to escort her.

"Absolutely, and that's only because of my prior commitment to a good deed," he quipped, and leaned over for a lightning-quick kiss on her temple. "My landlords put me to shame, though. Did I tell you Davis Calloway is a Gideon? His wife also talks to people she meets every day about the Lord, and they always have a New Testament ready to give away."

They stopped to look both ways on the quiet street, then Bijou watched Quincy to see if he moved ahead. She started the blur of her tiny paws when he took a step.

"No, you didn't mention it, but we have two Gideons in our church, and I love to hear their stories of unexpected ways Jesus used their willingness to serve. When I hear accounts like theirs and from the mission fields, I marvel at the supernatural ways the Lord brings about His will."

"I'm hoping to hear more of those this summer. They are busy and respectful of my privacy, knowing I'm working from the carriage house, so I don't get to see them as often as you see Lois. They have a home church, but they often travel around to speak on Sundays. Want to visit a church with me to hear them?"

"I'd love to," Mercedes said as another couple strolled past with a German Shepherd. They all smiled and wished each other a good evening while Bijou looked up at the dog who dwarfed her. The Shepherd barely acknowledged her.

"What about Bible study?" Quincy asked, bumping her gently with his shoulder. "I'm finishing up one online, through the book of Ezekiel, from the perspective of the Jewish understanding of the divine council in the book of Enoch. Are you interested in finding another one to start together?"

"Perfect timing," Mercedes replied, bumping her shoulder into his. "We finished Revelation with my group back in Charleston, then I came down here for the summer and jumped into a refresher in Scripture when Jana asked for my help on a topic. I listen to sermons and podcasts, but I'm looking for another study to do."

They enjoyed a leisurely stroll with Bijou until the paver walkway to her home was before them. Quincy scooped up the tiny dog to carry her to the glass storm door and she tried to lick his face for a sweet goodbye when he rang the bell. Her owner was there instantly to take her, accepting Bijou's happy kisses and thanking Quincy profusely. He turned to point to Mercedes on the sidewalk, introducing her as his girlfriend.

Bijou's owner waved at her and said, "You're even more lovely than he described. Thank you for helping with my Baby Bijou!"

Saying their goodbyes, Quincy glanced at his watch. "Have you been down to the dock and pier on Calhoun Street yet?

It's only a few blocks, and I hear the sunsets from there are stunning. Want to explore before we swim?"

"I've been meaning to go there myself, and you know I'm a sunset and moonlight kind of girl who can never resist exploring with you. It will be a good time to talk about the new job I'm working on in Savannah."

They paused for a crosswalk, where Quincy pulled a hand wipe out of a flat pack in his pocket. With a rapid pass of it over his hands to wipe traces of Bijou from them and not trigger Mercedes' allergies, he tossed it into a trash bin at the intersection. "Of course! I got sidetracked from asking about the job when I got you all to myself at lunch today, trying to win you back again. Okay, so start at when you showed up with police in front of the house. What was that all about?"

He reached for her hand to hold while they walked. She said, "The house is unusual, more like one I'd see in New Orleans—Creole Townhouse style with lots of lacy black ironwork on stacked porches, with Spanish and Caribbean influences. It's noticeable because of the Federal and Georgian styles on either side of it, and it's the only one like it on that street. The police were there because an intruder had a key to the back door and opened it last night. The clients who hired me are Tammy and Clayton Popplewell. Tammy believes the intruder came to their bedroom door and opened it. Clayton agrees they kept it closed for their room air conditioner to work and to keep out the musty smell of the house. But it was standing open when she woke him up. It terrified her."

They changed their pace, waiting on slower walkers ahead of them as they all walked toward the pier. Quincy said, "Before you answered me about why the police were there, you described the house. Does that mean the Creole influence is important?"

Mercedes hesitated. "I didn't realize I did that, but yes, the style made me wonder about the builder. I did some research this afternoon, and he was from New Orleans. He brought some servants with him when he moved his bride to Savannah in mid-eighteen hundred. When Tammy invited me into the house, one of the first things I saw—and felt—were some occult items in the shabby décor. I'm uncertain why I'm associating a connection with the superstitions of some of the Creoles and the history of the house, but just between us, it is nagging at me."

They went down a boardwalk to the end of the pier, where the sunset was about to become spectacular. Several other couples gathered with them, and Quincy stood behind her, wrapping his arms around her waist and looking over her shoulder. "It's breathtaking," she murmured.

They rocked with the pier like a slow dance in the wakes of passing boats. The exquisite colors of the skies proclaimed the glory of God, and like the other couples, they were too awed to speak. The May River became a liquid mirror of the sky colors and the marshy spartina grasses on the other side glowed as if illuminated from within.

When the shrinking half-circle kissed the horizon with a lingering goodbye, Quincy took her hand to walk back in romantic twilight. They turned up the boardwalk, where a sign proclaimed that Bluffton was a state of mind.

As they crossed the first street, he asked, "What evidence did the police find about the intruder at the Popplewell's house?"

"Footprints. Just bruised grass and dents in the sand. They led from the door to an old building in the back, which wasn't supposed to be there now. It should have been demolished before the Popplewell couple arrived, but the company left town with bad debts. The property managers and real estate agent are getting another company to handle it soon. There's a gate in sad condition behind a hedge in the backyard, and a bare area large enough for teens and kids to get through if they wanted to. The police think that's where the intruder came in. They don't know why there's interest in the old building or why someone has the back door key to the main house, but I noticed a rusty nail on the wall where a key could have been."

They reached the carriage house where Quincy lived, and she waited in a rocking chair outside the door while he changed into his swimsuit. Then they followed the sidewalk two houses up while Mercedes talked about the job in Savannah. "I didn't realize the old building in the back yard interested me until Clayton mentioned I seem drawn to it. My records call it the gardener's quarters. Then they showed me around inside the main house, and it's much larger than it looks from the road—deep, not wide. Some of the room measurements are too small. I believe there's a closed off area that was once a hallway."

"Like, a secret room?" Quincy asked, as she unlocked her cottage to go in and change.

"It's just a hunch. We'll see what the contractor says when I meet him day after tomorrow."

Quincy whistled and looked thoughtful as he went to sit in the nearest lounge chair to wait for her to change into her swimsuit. "Sounds fascinating. If I can rearrange my schedule, I'd like to tag along with you."

As she put her breakfast dishes in the dishwasher, Mercedes got a text notification on her cellphone. She dried her hands and went to pick it up. It was Tammy Popplewell. *Mercedes, can you possibly get here as soon as possible? A young neighbor stopped by, and she insists she must talk to you. She said I was not the lady in her dream last night and she needed to see the one with blonde hair. Creepy, huh? The cleaning service is here, and everything is chaos, but if you can come, Clayton will handle them, and we'll go out back and sit at the old patio table.*

Mercedes' heart jumped, and she reached for her cup of tea. She drank the last, wondering how to respond. The only thing on her calendar today was to do some laundry and work on research and paperwork for the Popplewell house, but she had hoped for a rare afternoon nap.

She hesitated, then responded. *Is she waiting? I can leave now, but it will take at least 45 minutes.*

The girl says it's important, and she will go do something at home and come back. I don't know what this is about, but I really appreciate you coming to handle this.

You're welcome, and I'll see you in a little while.

Mercedes sighed as she put down her phone and tapped her fingertips on the quartz countertop. An unsettled feeling sent her turning to prayer, reminding Jesus that she had given Him her day as a blank page to write on. She asked Him to prepare her for what was ahead and guide her to do things His way, not her own.

Next, she texted Quincy. He had an online meeting this morning, but she was uncertain what time. Then she rushed to slide on some shoes and gather her handbag and tablet, and when she picked up her phone to go out the door, he had not responded.

Quincy finally signed off from a longer-than-scheduled meeting and stretched his arms behind his head. Then he turned in his swivel office chair and reached for his cellphone to check messages. Mercedes was among them, so he opened her text first.

Good morning! Hope work is going well. I just wanted to ask for prayer for an unusual turn in my schedule today. Tammy Popplewell asked me to come to Savannah right away. A neighbor, a young girl, showed up there at the house this morning and said she must speak to the lady with blonde hair that was in her dreams last night.

The office chair rolled backwards and almost toppled over when Quincy shot to his feet, staring at the phone in his hand and re-reading Mercedes' message. Then, he went to stand in front of a window with a scenic view of his landlord's garden. His mind, and his heart, raced too much to compose more than a jumbled prayer right now.

He looked at the message again, then texted back. *Honey, you don't know how much I've missed these adrenaline rushes! Life without you didn't just make my heart ache, it was downright boring. I missed wondering if mummies were going to come to life or if the suit of armor in a castle was going to come after me with a battleax. This is the life I came here to have. I'll start praying right now. Let me know if everything is okay or if you need me to drive there.*

Mercedes made her way through the front door of the Popplewell house, dodging the cleaning service employees and their roaring equipment. She escaped into the kitchen and saw Tammy gathering a tray of snacks.

"Oh, hi, Mercedes! Are you hungry? I was just getting something to take outside."

"No, thanks. I have a bottle of water and just ate breakfast. Can I help you carry anything?"

"I think I have it all, but you can get the door. Our guest is here. Her name is Tonya."

The back door had a new handle and lock, Mercedes noticed as she opened it for Tammy, and a girl of about eleven or twelve sat swinging her lanky legs from a seat on the rusty metal patio furniture. She wore her hair in perfect braids and bright beads.

The moment her eyes rested on Mercedes, she gasped and put both hands to her mouth. Mercedes smiled and went to sit beside her as Tammy set down the tray and offered her refreshments. She stared wide-eyed at Mercedes, who said, "Hi, Tonya, it's such a pleasure to meet you. My name is Mercedes Ellison. Won't you have something to eat?"

Tonya gulped and nodded. "Mercedes? Like the car?"

Mercedes laughed. "Yes, but it means something nice. I'm named after my Great-Great Grand Aunt, and I found her diary recently in an old cedar chest, so I'm getting to know her, though she's in heaven. Our name is Spanish for 'mercies.' My middle name is Annalee. Anna is Hebrew for 'grace' or 'favor' and Lee means 'meadow.' Are you named after any relatives in your family?"

Tonya shook her head and said no, her mama just thought it was a pretty name. She tore her eyes from Mercedes to reach for a cookie and a cup of icy fruit punch. She thanked Tammy politely and took a big bite of the sugar cookie, looking back at Mercedes. When she swallowed, she asked, "Don't you want a cookie, too?"

"I wish I could have one, but some foods make me get sick. I have to eat specially made cookies."

"Oh. I've heard of some people being like that." Tonya sipped some of her drink.

"Tonya, tell Mercedes about your dream," said Tammy, putting another cookie in front of the girl.

Once again, Tonya studied Mercedes. In a thick local accent, she said, "It was my Granny. She said I need to come talk about my dream and the things I know. She lives through that gate back there and looks after me when school is out, but I'm big enough not to have a babysitter."

"Maybe it's good to be with her, though, in case she needs you," ventured Mercedes. "Did the police visit her yesterday?"

"Yeah, but I was out with my friends. We went up to the corner store for things Granny had on a list, and she gave us extra money to buy popsicles. It was powerful hot yesterday. Granny told the police some things about who goes through the gate, but she didn't tell them about this house. I'm supposed to tell you, that's what my dream was. No one said to tell you, like some scary voice. I just knew. And I didn't really see your face, mostly your hair, and I knew you had eyes like a meadow, the way your name says."

Mercedes blinked in surprise. This description reminded her of how her Great-Great Grand Aunt Mercedes described her beloved grandmother, Claire. "How lovely," she breathed. Then she said, "Is it all right if Tammy hears what you want to tell me? She will live here in the house when we finish all the work."

Tonya glanced at Tammy. "Since she wasn't in my dream, is it okay if I just tell you, and you can tell her? I want to do this right."

Tammy smiled and reached to pat Tonya's hand. "I'll come back when you're finished. I should go inside with Clayton and be sure the house is getting cleaned right."

Chapter 3

Tonya swallowed another bite of her cookie and turned a solemn expression to Mercedes. "Miss Mercedes, I'll tell you what I know first, and then say what my Granny knows. It's okay, she told me to, and I'm not tellin' secrets. My family has known things about this house for a long time, see. My big sister and my cousin, they meet up with some friends here sometimes and one older boy has a key. He told my sister he found it at that old building, back there." Tonya turned and pointed to the ramshackle gardener's quarters.

"Tonya, I want to interrupt for a minute in case I forget to tell you this. That building is truly dangerous to be around. It's a matter of life and death for you to warn your sister and her friends not to break inside it. Can I count on you to warn them?"

The girl nodded. "Yes, and my Granny has told them, too. But the older boy, he wanted the key the spirit told him to get. Enough people's been killed here already."

Mercedes' heart skipped a beat, and she felt breathless. Gaining composure and mulling over what to say next, she took a drink of water from a clear insulated bottle with a kayaking adventure logo on it. It was getting hot and muggy, even in the patio's shade.

"Tonya, does the boy who has the key encounter spirits often, and is that how he learned about the killings that happened here on the property?"

With a scowl of distaste, the girl explained. "I think he does that kind of thing anyway, but I know he does it here, in the front room. He has this we-a-gee board, and some other spooky stuff, and he comes here when the moon is full. My sister and cousin got terrified last time, though. See, he's handsome and popular at school, and they want to be around him and his friends. So, they sneaked out late at night from Granny's and came through that gate behind her house. They stole two of Granny's emergency candles 'cause the boy wanted everyone to bring something. They told me what happened, 'cause they had to confess to Granny, since they brought back a spirit with them to her house and she needed to pray in every room to make it leave."

Now, Mercedes struggled to disguise her alarm. In a silent prayer, she asked for wisdom. "So, the last time there was a full moon, your sister and cousin gathered here in the front living room with friends, and they lit candles and called on spirits using the board. Did your sister say if the boy she admires has the same spirit that followed her home?"

"Yes, ma'am, they came here, and they had a bottle of powerful stuff to drink, too. One boy stole it from his parents. But the spirit that usually comes for the leader differs from the one that tagged on my sister and cousin. It's like a boss spirit, and he calls him 'Papa' something."

Mercedes' knuckles tightened on the edge of her seat as her mind raced. *Voodoo.*

"When my sister and cousin got scared and ran out the back door, they stopped to unlatch the gate. That thing was behind them and had a wicked face, they said. They covered their mouths to keep from screaming, and they ran to Granny's, waking her up by pounding on the back door. They clung to her in horror, crying, and told her what happened.

Every time they turned, that thing was behind them, grinning. I got up too, with all the ruckus, and that's how I know all this. My Granny didn't fuss at them right off, she just said, what did you expect, calling on things like that, which no Christian should do, and she sat them down at the kitchen table. She got out her Bible and started prayin' up a storm, and I mean that. It was goin' to storm anyway, said the weatherman, but it started for certain while she prayed over my sister and cousin, over the doors, over the windows, and every room. She even went out in the storm and prayed over the yard and that gate 'til the rain started."

"Did the spirit leave?"

"O'course it did. They got no chance when my Granny calls on Jesus. She had her prayer group and our pastor out the next day, too, prayin' over everything, but there was nothing around. And you can bet my sister and cousin won't be back here. They aren't who the police are lookin' for 'bout the other night."

Mercedes nodded, watching Tonya sip the last of her fruit punch. She reached for the pitcher in a bucket of melting ice and poured a little more into the girl's cup. They were both wilting in the sweltering heat. "Tonya, tell me about who died here."

"My Granny's family has a story, only it's true, not a yarn, mind you. It's written in some old diaries she used to have, but the family, they always tell the next kids that are born, like me and my sister. My mom, she don't hold much to it. But back in the bad war that happened here in Savannah, the family who built this house abandoned it for a safer place. There was no way to take the servants. They were like most, didn't have slaves, but they liked their servant folks and Granny says they all cried to be parted. The family gave them money to last 'til they could go get jobs or join one of the two armies, but Granny's people stayed on in town, hopin' to watch over the house and that the owners could return when the army left. One was the gardener, and he looked over the grounds, which were beautiful. Another was his sister, and she was a housemaid. She was beautiful, too."

"Are they the ones who lived in the building back here?"

Tonya nodded. "First, his sister lived in the big house with the family and stayed until some carpetbagger named Jack Haute took over it after the war. He was a mean one, and a swindler. He committed a bunch of thefts and murders in town, but there was no law to protect locals from the Yankees. Granny said he could charm a snake, though, and Sirena became his girlfriend. He said the family she worked for was probably dead and would never return, and that he owned the house now. He promised to make her mistress of it someday. But he made her live in the gardener's cottage with her brother. Her brother was furious 'bout her bein' Jack's girlfriend, but he held his peace so he could be near his sister. One night, Sirena sneaked out to go meet Jack in the house, and he was with another woman. She saw them from the bedroom door and knew the woman was the wife of a leader in the city, and she was jealous. Her brother heard from the open windows and came to stand outside his door to listen to where the argument was coming from. He heard his sister say a powerful curse over them and she threatened to go tell the woman's husband. Then he heard her scream. But it stopped as if he hit her. He went to the door, but his sister had locked it behind her, so he tried to get in windows. He didn't have a weapon and Jack pointed a gun at him, sayin' he was breaking in and he had a right to shoot him. Jack ordered him to get off the property. So, her brother, he ran to find help, but no one wanted to deal with Jack, and they scorned Sirena as a fool who got what she deserved. The law wouldn't come back with him to help find her. No one would come until the next day, and Jack lied about even bein' here that night. But no one ever saw Sirena after that."

Mercedes scowled. "Since there was no justice for Sirena, her brother got revenge, didn't he?"

With a nod, Tonya said, "Yes. He told his relations that he took care of old Jack Haute, and the devil had him. But he never found his sister, and he left for New Orleans."

"Tonya, are you upset by this story? Do you ever get scared?"

The girl sipped her cold drink and grinned. "Oh, no, Miss Mercedes. I'm saved by the blood of Jesus, and hallelujah, as Granny says! The real-life stuff I hear at school is worse than the story of Sirena and Jack. But the boy who came here and called on spirits during the full moon, when my sister and cousin were here to see it, that scares me a little. People like that, they do what the spirits say, like murder and worse, and Jesus allows bad things to happen to His people sometimes. Granny says we don't know the reasons, but we will someday. Granny also says Sirena and her brother didn't have true faith. They came from voodoo superstitions and mixed them with some Christian things, like calling their spirits by the Catholic saints' names. That boy my sister thought she loved called his spirit a strange name my Granny says is voodoo."

"Will your sister stay away from that boy now?"

Tonya rolled her eyes. "For certain! The evil spirit with the hideous face made her want to obey my Granny from now on. She said no boy's worth all that."

Mercedes walked Tonya to the gate and said goodbye, then she carried Tammy's tray from the patio to the kitchen. She stood before the air conditioner, letting the soft breeze dry her skin. There was no hope for the damp waistband of her shorts and underarms of her tank top.

Tammy opened the door to the rest of the house and stopped short in surprise. She pulled the door closed and went to the refrigerator for fresh ice and bottled water, telling Mercedes to pull a chair up to the struggling little air conditioning unit.

Wiping sweat from her own brow after being in the hot, musty house, she said, "You've gone above and beyond the call of duty for me and Clayton, sweetheart. I hope what Tonya had to say is worth nearly having a heat stroke for."

"Oh, yes, it was. But what do I do with that information now? That's always my dilemma. Unusual information gets plopped in my path so I can't ignore it, then I must sort through it and pray. The best news for you and Clayton is that your back door neighbors are faithful Christians. At least, the grandmother and Tonya are. The bad news is that bad things have apparently occurred on the property."

Tammy sat down in one of the painted metal kitchen chairs and blew out a breath. She dabbed a napkin over her broad brow and said, "I knew it! Let me have it."

"I'll keep this to a nutshell version until we act on specifics. First, a young man has the key to the old lock on the back door, so it's good that Clayton changed the lock. The teen claims to have been acting on the guidance of a spirit when he went to find it at the gardener's quarters out back. However, we must factor in that he was likely under the influence of another spirit from a bottle. Strong drink doesn't guide people to keys, but it can make them do foolish things, like go to the old building and find a key, then brag to friends that a spirit told him where to find it."

"I see. There may or may not be haunting going on."

"Not a haunting, as many people think of it, because spirits of deceased humans can't remain trapped on earth. But he was gathering friends here sometimes, especially on nights with a full moon, and they were delving into occult things. He may have learned about them from books, movies, video games, or online. Tonya's older sister likes the popular young man. She and her cousin sneaked out of their grandmother's home, behind your house, and came through the gate to meet the others. They brought candles, someone else brought a bottle of booze, and she didn't know what items other participants brought. I suspect some objects you are clearing out of the front room are among those. At some point, he used a Ouija board to conjure up spirits better left alone, and sure enough, Tonya's sister and cousin became terrified by whatever happened. They claim that a spirit with a hideous face stuck close to them and they bolted from the house to the gate, and as they unlatched it, they turned to see the spirit was following them home."

Tammy's eyes were wide, and she clapped a hand to her mouth. Mercedes let her consider all the information so far, sipping ice water. When Tammy took her hand from her mouth and told Mercedes to go on, she continued.

"Tonya says a 'ruckus' awakened her when her sister and cousin banged on the back door, begging their grandmother to let them in. She did, and they claimed they could still see the spirit staying near them. Granny knows how to deal with this kind of thing and went for her Bible and the power of Jesus in prayer. She prayed over the girls, the openings to the house, all the rooms, and then went outside in a storm to clear the yard all the way to your gate. Tonya says the house is peaceful and demon-free to this day. But her sister and cousin learned a lesson that Granny could never have taught them with a warning."

Tammy rubbed her hands over her face and Mercedes gently asked if she was okay. She nodded and asked if the girls' grandmother told the police this.

"Tonya's Granny told them about how some kids use the gate to get into the back yard and that she has heard of them having seances and doing other occult things on the property when the house is empty. She didn't tell them about her granddaughter's experience. Honestly, Tammy, while we can see Granny was very serious about how she handled the evil spirit, there's the possibility that the girls were also under the influence of alcohol and overactive imaginations."

Tammy looked a bit shaken as she sipped iced tea and reached for the last sugar cookie left on the tray for Tonya. "We don't have to worry about the teens coming back now, and we will soon live in the house."

Mercedes nodded. "I think that part of the story is over, yes. But there's another one, an older one, and unfortunately, it seems to be supported by my research on the house. Do you want me to tell you about it with Clayton around?"

With a wave of her hand, Tammy dismissed waiting on Clayton. "He's frustrated with the cleaning crew and isn't in the mood for house history. He'll be a bear by the time those people leave. Just tell me, and he can talk to you about it tomorrow when the contractor comes."

Mercedes told Tonya's account of Sirena, her brother, and Jack Haute. Tammy stared at her when it was over. "Do you believe this happened?"

"I believe it is possible, and sadly, not even unusual for those times. Heaven knows how many other places in the city this kind of thing, and worse, took place in such a lawless situation. What I don't know is, if it is true, where are the bodies?"

Chapter 4

Mercedes used the remote start on her key fob to get the air conditioning turned on before she even made it to her Jeep. The heat rose from the black asphalt street to the sidewalk, draining her energy and enthusiasm. She sank gratefully into the pale leather driver's seat, adjusting the air vents to blow directly on her. Her face was flushed pink, and she reached into the cup holder for an elastic band to pull her hair up into a messy bun.

Before pulling from her parking place, she took a minute to check messages on her phone. She smiled to see Quincy had left several messages. It had been a long time since he called her Honey, and it was good to see he was straightforward about the heartache he experienced during the past year. The time stamp on the text revealed he sent it as she was going into the Popplewell's house, so he had been praying for her when it counted most. Half an hour later, he was checking in to see if everything was okay. And recently, he said to call him.

The call button was on her steering wheel, and she pressed it as she glanced in the mirror. The air conditioning had blown away the heat flush on her cheeks. She told the vehicle connection service to call Quincy, and it started ringing his phone. He picked up on the first ring.

"Hi, Quincy."

"There you are! Is everything okay?"

"I think so, but I have some unusual stuff to sort through. Thanks so much for praying! I'm leaving Savannah now. I'm drained from being in the heat and having a lot on my mind, so I'm planning to have a nap when I get to the cottage."

He sighed. "You're not eating lunch?"

"Maybe an apple from the countertop basket on the way to lay down on the sofa."

"All right, sleeping beauty, let me know when you wake up. Let's get takeout somewhere and eat dinner by the pool tonight if the weather holds up. Sounds like you have a lot to tell me."

"I do, and it's weird, I can say that. Brace yourself. I need a logical perspective to ground me. Looking forward to later."

"Me too. My best times are with you."

Quincy admired Mercedes as she sat across from him at Lois's patio table. She looked rested, but she was solemn and distracted during dinner. "I'm stuffed," she announced, sitting back. "That was delicious! Thanks a million for dinner. I love it when you do the cooking."

"Me, too," he said, patting his stomach. "I'm stuffed, I mean. There are so many good places to eat around here. As for doing the cooking, I enjoy taking care of you. Ordering dinner out was the obvious thing to do tonight."

"Can we lounge by the pool in the chairs for a while? I think a storm is coming."

"That's a great idea. Go on and pick out a seat while I throw these containers in the outdoor trash bin."

Pines and oaks rustled over the courtyard as a gusty breeze stirred the branches. Clouds sagged with humidity, promising rain to quench the thirst of heat-baked plants. Quincy hoped he would have an hour with Mercedes before the storm. At this point in their relationship, and with Lois and the Calloways watching as their landlord chaperones, it was tricky to spend innocent time together in her cottage or his carriage house apartment. His parents brought him up on the biblical concept of avoiding even the appearance of participating in sin, whether in the places he went or things he did with friends, or situations he was in with women. Watching his friends' lives, he knew even people who had no faith were better off when they were careful to avoid secluded situations, for American culture was all about accusations and lawsuits. For now, staying outside in the evenings and going to public places was best for his relationship with Mercedes. He would guard it and protect her from gossip and speculation.

He reached into his duffle bag on a nearby chair and pulled out two pretty gift bags, then went to sit by Mercedes, who had started some soft instrumental music on her phone and pulled his lounge chair next to hers. Stretching out on it, he made himself comfortable and watched her eyes sparkle in curiosity when she saw the bags.

Quincy cleared his throat. "It's official. Bijou's mommy has relieved me of my service, though she may call upon me in extreme circumstances. Therefore, you are the only girl in my life and have all my attention. But you may want a token of your one and only walk with Bijou."

Mercedes laughed and peeked into the shimmering lavender bag he gave her, which looked so much like one of Bijou's leashes. But he expected her peeking and had rolled the gift in extra metallic pink tissue filler, which she pulled out. When she unwrapped the gift, the look on her face was worth all the trouble of searching online for it.

"Oh," she breathed. "Quincy, it's like Bijou! I love it! Thank you so much."

He watched her pat back the ruffled fur of the tiny pocket-sized stuffed animal and finger the jeweled collar. With a full heart, he said, "This one is allergy-friendly, takes up almost no space, doesn't shed, and is cheap to own. You can keep your health, independence, and your budget, while the real animals in your life are born free and run wild. I know it bothers you that breeders of designer pets deform dogs and make them live with chronic health issues."

The look she turned to him made his heart flip over. "I'm thrilled with this little reminder that I'm the only woman in your life now, and you know you're the only man in mine."

Deeply touched, he reached out to run his hand over her arm. She leaned over to brush a light kiss on his neck. "It's really a sweet gift and you're a sweet guy to think of it," she murmured.

He was trying to get over the effect of that kiss on his neck when he handed her the second bag. She studied the whimsical ocean theme design, then reached inside. When she unwrapped the gift tissue paper, she found a painted tile art panel depicting two swimming dolphins.

Her expression turned emotional, and he wondered if it was too soon for this gift. She covered her mouth and squeezed her eyes shut, but only for a few moments. Then she held the picture up, letting the light set off the raised outlines of the dolphins, waves, and bubbles in the design. "It's more than beautiful. I'll always treasure this. I don't think people will believe the story when it comes out, but I know it happened."

"I saw it, too. It was no dream. God doesn't bless many people with such miraculous answers to prayer. I almost lost you without ever sharing my heart and telling you I was here. Every day since, I've praised the Lord for what He did that night. Even the animals obey His will. And He used the wild and free animals to rescue you."

He reached for her hand, and she put down the fragile tile. "Let's stand up," she murmured, and they did. She pulled him close, and they hugged, swaying to the ambient music like a slow dance by the glowing turquoise pool. The brass lanterns sparkled warmly, insect wings buzzed, and in the distance, thunder rumbled.

"It wasn't just the dolphins who rescued me that night, Quincy. They brought me as far as they could. The Lord arranged for you to be there, too."

Quincy hugged her tighter and whispered, "Yes, He did. That honor is another reason I praise Him. If I didn't already know how much you meant to me, I knew it then."

They swayed to the music a few more moments, and he said, "I could do this all night, but a storm is coming, and I'll have to leave, unless you want to sit on Lois' front porch swing under the roof. Do you want to tell me about what happened to you today, or shall I call you on the phone after I get home?"

She stopped swaying and pulled away, leading him by the hand back to their chairs. The thunder was closer as she finished her version of all that happened, and she asked for his thoughts.

"I cleared my work schedule tomorrow and I'm going with you to the Popplewell house. It will be easier to have an informed opinion after looking the place over, but let's suppose the remains of Sirena and Haute are on the premises. Are you prepared to deal with that?"

"I can call authorities, but I hope the contractors will be the ones to make any discoveries. I'm hired to do tedious paperwork and give advice. They dig and smash and build and have a government protocol to follow in the event of finding bones and remains."

Quincy sighed. "Okay. But aside from the legalities, what about your emotions? And if this plays out, Tammy and Clayton will need to cope. Frankly, a discovery like this, dating around the end of the Civil War, will make the property more valuable. True drama will make them a featured stop on the haunted tours of Savannah and put the house in the museums and tour books, and if they open an inn, it will be popular. But about the girl's dream, Mercedes, I can't just dismiss that, and you shouldn't, either. As far as the claims of the teen who has a key to the house and the girl's sister and cousin—we can rationalize it by assuming they drank too much, and heaven knows what else they consumed and didn't mention. Where do we stop assuming this is their imagination and accept that they may have encountered something real?"

Mercedes showered and dressed early the next morning, ready to face whatever the day brought. She wanted to look professional but needed to be cool and casual in the stifling heat. Tammy would text her with the schedule for the contractor's arrival, and she and Quincy planned to ride down and tour the city by car so he could see it for the first time. She was finishing a gluten-free half a bagel with dairy-free cream cheese and a small strawberry-pineapple smoothie when she got Tammy's update.

Brad says he will be here this morning by nine-thirty. Clayton and I will be there at nine to open the house up.

Mercedes sent a message back to her. *Is Brad the contractor's name? Yes, I will be there shortly after nine, and I'm bringing a friend today. His name is Quincy Holmwood.*

Tammy was quick with her message back to Mercedes. *Yes, the contractor's name is Brad. Supposed to be best at historic remodeling and restoration. The property management agency screened contractors for us and took quotes. They were all about the same amount, but this company has the best reputation.*

Okay, Quincy and I will see you soon.

Next, Mercedes texted Quincy, who said he was on his way.

Quincy put the Savannah destination in his car navigation system while a yacht rock station flowed through the speakers on satellite radio. Mercedes showed him landmarks and points of historic interest along the way, including Lafayette Square, which was within walking distance of the Popplewell house. Tammy and Clayton welcomed them into a bare shell of the enormous residence, now free of clutter, ruined furniture, dry-rotted draperies, and broken chandeliers.

They barely finished introductions for Quincy when Brad arrived and rang the doorbell, which weakly warbled. Clayton opened the doors again and invited Brad into the cavernous entryway and front living room space. They made introductions again, and Brad studied Mercedes before looking around him. Quincy gave her hand a jealous squeeze.

"Come on in. We got things cleared out yesterday, so it may be easier to see anything you missed last time," said Clayton, who was all smiles and cheerful mood.

Brad stepped forward and looked around. "Yes, it was a wreck before you took over. Nasty stuff going on in this room, kids messin' around. It's a miracle they didn't set the place on fire."

"You know about that?" blurted Tammy, wide-eyed.

"Yeah, got a good friend in law enforcement," Brad said, walking into the kitchen. "We're gonna gut this part, right?"

"Right," answered Clayton. "You have the plans? Mercedes—uh, Miss Ellison is here if you want to ask her questions about them."

Brad glanced at Mercedes and nodded before turning his attention back to the house. "Yeah, in the truck if I need 'em. I'm mainly concerned with the soundness of the structure right now and what we have to work with."

Warped boards protested under his work boots as he examined the gloomy downstairs hallway and opened the bedroom where the Popplewells had hoped to stay. The group followed him around while he interacted with Clayton.

"Where's the basement door?" asked Brad.

Clayton wore a blank look. Mercedes had her tablet open to the paperwork on the property and said, "I expected a basement or at least a small cellar, as well. The original records on this house were lost during the American Civil War, and there is never a basement mentioned on the legal paperwork between buyers once the builders abandoned it, presumably about 1865 or 1866."

Brad scowled. "People back then, they put up canned and dried goods. Stored stuff. The first time I was here, there was so much old furniture in this area I assumed they had moved a large piece in front of the door. I'll look again on the outside. Maybe there's a step-down entrance."

They followed the contractor through shadows up the wide staircase, turning on a creaky landing floor to twist up to the second floor. He roamed around from room to room. "The measurements don't add up," he said matter-of-factly, his voice echoing in the emptiness.

"That's exactly what Mercedes—uh, Miss Ellison—said when she looked things over," said Clayton.

Mercedes went to the wall she felt was sealed off. "Right here. There should be a hallway here, open like a balcony or landing by the staircase. It may have been closed to make a closet or other storage, but then, where is the door? It created an abnormal flow to the way these two rooms should have opened. People must go through one room to get to the other, and the rooms lack any closets. Occupants probably used a wardrobe."

Brad studied her again. "You knew my evaluation would agree with yours."

She kept her eyes on his. "Yes, if you were a contractor who knows anything about historical restoration."

He bit his lip. "What do you expect me to find?"

She drew a deep breath. "If there is anything but space, you'll know before I do."

His mouth quirked now, as if he fought a grin. "Not if you're here when I open it up."

He spun on his boot heel and went toward a small door in the hall. "Attic stairs?" he asked Clayton.

"Yes, and it was all cleared out yesterday. Careful, it needs a new floor."

Mercedes turned a furtive look at Quincy, who made an elusive gesture of pointing at himself. If she was there when Brad opened the wall, he would be with her.

When Brad finished in the house, he walked around the grounds. He questioned Clayton about the old gardener's quarters, said he could get someone out quickly to take it down, then examined the weatherworn exterior of the residence. All the while, he was making suggestions to Clayton, which Mercedes noted on her tablet. She stood with Quincy in the shade of a sprawling, melancholy oak that dripped Spanish moss, close enough to hear without being part of the conversation. She whispered to him that time seemed to crawl on sweltering summer days.

The contractor finally announced that he saw no evidence of a cellar or basement entrance, but the covered small windows and grill vents in the foundation were evidence that one existed. He would get someone out to clear away the tangle of choking vines that may hide an entrance. Tammy wiped sweat from her forehead and glanced at Mercedes before turning back to him. "Honestly, at this point, I expect to discover a dungeon with moldering skeletons dangling in chains from the walls."

Mercedes laughed out loud. Brad looked startled, then chuckled with Clayton while they all went gratefully into the kitchen, where the room air conditioning offered tepid relief.

"I'll go to the truck to write up some paperwork about the job, to get things on schedule," said Brad. "Call your agent or the property management agency if you want my team over right away to bring down the outdoor building. Honestly, I need that space cleared to store building materials, so the sooner it's finished, the sooner we get to work. Are you livin' here?"

Clayton looked down at Tammy, who flushed from the heat. "We've been sleeping at a nearby weekly stay hotel until we figure that out. The first night, we had an intruder. I changed the locks, and all the musty furniture and rugs are gone, so we may move back if we won't be in your way. Just thought it would be easier for everyone if we were on site when you needed us."

Brad nodded. "That works for now, but you'll want to leave when I start in the kitchen. You can move things into an area I'll finish with if you decide to stay on site. Questions for me?"

Clayton followed the contractor out, asking about the timeline for what they would accomplish first. Tammy offered Mercedes and Quincy refreshments. "I have a snack you can eat, Mercedes," she said, and pulled out popsicles made of organic pineapple and mango juice, sweetened with apple and white grape juices.

Mercedes was so moved that she hugged Tammy, despite their clammy, cooling skin. "That was unbelievably thoughtful of you! Thanks, I'll devour one right now."

She took the offered popsicle, and Quincy asked for the same. Tammy provided a roll of paper towels in case of any sticky drips, and all three of them acted like kids with popsicles on a summer day. They sat on the cool metal of the vintage chairs at the table.

"Quincy, what do you think of the property?" asked Tammy as they enjoyed the icy treats.

Mercedes smiled as he discretely dabbed a paper towel at his mouth. Little things like that were billboards for his aristocratic upbringing, and Tammy was noticing. He replied, "It's even more interesting than Mercedes described. I'm used to digging for things, so I admit I'm intrigued about the possibility of a missing cellar. Now that I've seen the upstairs mystery about the space not adding up, I'll be watching to see what happens there. But the outside is going to have a lot of personality, and you should have a unique inn that visitors will flock to."

"Quincy grew up functioning as an archaeologist on dig sites, home educating with his family and getting a degree in the field," Mercedes told Tammy. "His family is from both England and the States, but he's here to stay now, working in Antiquities for collectors, fraud investigation, museums, and places like that."

Tammy licked the last chunk of her popsicle off the wooden stick, dabbed her mouth, then said, "I could tell you weren't from around here. That's fascinating! What a wonderful way to grow up! You have a slight British accent, but with a little of everywhere thrown in. Well, you may dig or hunt for anything here that you have a hunch about. You two look so cute together—I hope you're a couple."

Mercedes blushed and Quincy grinned. "Yes, ma'am, Mercedes is my girl. Has been for as long as I can remember, and her family has tagged along with mine in interesting places. She and her brother have some food allergies that make traveling abroad difficult. She can't live on archaeology sites long because of it. But the world changed dramatically from the way we and our parents grew up, so I had to pray about what to do with my career. Now I'm staying here to be with her, and I can't imagine any other life."

After saying goodbye to Tammy Popplewell, Mercedes and Quincy let themselves out through the front door, almost bumping face to face with Clayton on the front porch. He was all excitement, saying Brad had already called the property management company and gotten approval and the paperwork for a demolition of the decrepit old building in the back yard. A company he worked with was on the way and expected to finish and haul off the debris that afternoon, making room for Brad's materials to be stored in that spot. Another crew was delayed on a job and he coordinated for them to clear away brambles and vines around the exterior of the property, giving him and his crew easy access to the building.

"So much is happening! Brad was a splendid choice for this job," Mercedes told him. "Quincy and I are going to tour Savannah today and have lunch on the waterfront. Will you have Tammy text me when the old building is down? I can come back by here if you need me."

"Oh, sure, I'll do that."

Mercedes and Quincy stepped off the brick porch to the sidewalk, and Brad was by his truck a few parking spots away. He ended a phone call and waved to them to wait, then he hurried up, removing a ball cap with the construction company logo, and wiping sweat from his brow with his forearm. He settled the cap back on his short brown hair and said, "Miss Ellison, I didn't want to mention it in front of the Popplewell couple, but I have a friend in law enforcement who knows some stories about this house and has seen your name, and your family's name, pop up from time to time in solving cold cases and a sprinkle of—uh—paranormal cases. Glad to see you here."

Mercedes glanced at Quincy, then back to Brad. She smiled and said, "I don't look for that kind of excitement in my life, Brad. My clients choose me, and after an interview to see if they're the sort of people I can work with, I take the job. The clock ticks on research after I'm hired, when I can charge for my time, so I know next to nothing about any circumstances beforehand. Since I work with old properties, and people are what they are throughout history, evidence of crime occasionally happens on my job sites. You're in construction, so you know it's not uncommon to dig up skeletons."

He kept a steady gaze on her as she paused, cleared her throat, and continued. "As a Christian, I pray over my business. I honestly prefer quiet, boring properties, but sometimes unusual things come to light when I'm in charge. My clients rely on me to see them through, from my experience, and since I'm only twenty-five, that's not a lot in their favor. I do the best I can and leave the rest for Jesus."

Brad nodded, sighed, and said, "Glad to hear that. I'm a Christian, too, and it'll be interestin' to see what the Lord has led us to do here with the Popplewell house."

"Since the first time I saw the property on Monday morning, I can't get the gardener's quarters off my mind," Mercedes said. "There were tracks leading to it from the back door when I arrived, but your law enforcement friend probably told you more than I know about it. I don't want to presume to suggest how to do your job, but if you'll be supervising the demolition, do you mind being alert to anything unusual?"

Brad grinned. "Now we're gettin' somewhere! You can count on it. The crew will be here soon."

Quincy said, "We're going to lunch on the riverfront, then enjoying the sights around town today. Have Tammy contact Mercedes if there's any way we can help."

The men shook hands and Brad nodded goodbye to Mercedes. When she and Quincy got into his car, he looked over at her with a smile and tried out Brad's Southern accent. "Give me an address for that there restaurant, darlin'. We need a full stomach for an interestin' afternoon."

Savannah Jazz
Inspired by a photo I took of a musician playing for visitors
along the riverfront in Savannah, Georgia.
Pamela Poole

Chapter 5

Mercedes laughed often as she showed Quincy around the Savannah Riverfront. He was interested in the patchwork repairs on masonry and historic buildings. They walked cobblestone streets and ate local seafood in a restored 1850s cotton warehouse, where Mercedes reminded him that the building and the Popplewell house were new at about the same time in history. Then they browsed a shop of unique handmade crafts, where she bought a sea-scented candle in a shell-encrusted vase. When they passed the window of a gallery exhibiting the work of local artists, Quincy asked her if she was still painting.

"Not really. This past year, I buried myself in work, establishing an independent business so I'd be free from all the nonsense and discrimination in the workplace."

He squeezed her hand. "It's good to know I was your inspiration, and nothing was the same in a year without me."

They laughed together, then she said, "Yes, it's true. I didn't feel creative, but things are different now. Soon, I'll paint again."

Ahead of them, a man skillfully played a jazz melody on a saxophone in the park area. His music attracted a crowd that found shelter in the shade of the crooked branches of aging oaks. Quincy pointed and said, "Now there's a subject worthy of painting in a picturesque setting. I like the warm color of the saxophone against his skin and the distorted reflections on it."

They found a place to stand where Mercedes could get a photo with her cellphone camera, arranging the composition in her picture as well as she could. "You're right, this would make a great painting, if I can pull it off."

"You can pull it off, all right. Maybe after this busy week with the Popplewell job Brad can take over and you'll have some time to relax and paint something—assuming I don't hog up all your time for myself, which is tempting."

"I want to go bike riding and kayaking, so expect me to ask for an escort. Let's get out of the heat. Are you ready for a ride around to see some of the park squares? They have monuments, sculptures, and fountains. And the architecture is quaint and fascinating!"

"It's great to have a personal tour guide, and such a beautiful one, at that. Can we walk around an old cemetery?"

The heat rose without mercy from the concrete and asphalt of Savannah, keeping Mercedes and Quincy in his convertible with the top on and the air conditioning running. His car crept by the views as she pointed out the scenic park squares and historic sites, and they planned to do a walking tour when the weather was cooler. When she guided him to the old Colonial Park cemetery, she asked if he wanted to take some time to look around.

"We should take another day to go visit Bonaventure Cemetery, maybe in autumn. But this one is interesting, too. There are over nine thousand graves on six acres, and this was the main cemetery from 1750 to 1853, so if you can read any epitaphs, they may be memorable. It suffered a lot from vandalism during the Union occupation here and it's believed that soldiers changed the dates on some memorial stones."

Quincy was parking in the shade when Mercedes' cellphone notified her of a text message. She cupped it in her hand and squinted, turning the screen to eliminate reflections. "It's Tammy."

"Everything okay?"

Mercedes turned to him and almost whispered, "There are human remains under the floor of the gardener's quarters."

In a quick phone call to Tammy, Mercedes and Quincy learned they would only be in the way if they drove back to the Popplewell house. The authorities were protecting the evidence at the gardener's quarters. They sent a coroner and an archaeologist to examine the skeleton and verify the next steps.

Mercedes turned on the speakerphone so Quincy could hear. "Tammy, you sound shaky, and little wonder. Are you okay? I can come by if you need to talk when the crowd clears away from the house. And if you have questions that aren't answered about what happens with those remains and why an archaeologist came, Quincy can help. I have you on speaker phone now if you want to ask."

Tammy said she was going indoors to sit down to get away from the investigation. They heard a metal chair scrape the floor of the kitchen. "Yes, I'm rattled by the discovery. Yet, I'm not really surprised. Clayton reminded me of how you seemed to know something was off about that building from the moment you saw it, and after the story Tonya told us, I should have braced myself. Brad and Clayton are handling questions on the sidelines, and they will fill me in later. But if Quincy has a dummies version, I would like to hear it."

Quincy's tone was gentle. "Tammy, it's not as uncommon as you may think for human remains to be found on construction sites, and for various reasons. When a project manager calls authorities in those cases, state laws have guidelines for how to handle the remains. A coroner will determine things like the cause of death, and if he suspects the remains have been around for a long time, an archaeologist examines anything that will help determine the year or era of the death before the construction work can resume. Someone must remove the remains right away to preserve the evidence. After the investigation, they will bury the body in a proper place. Unless this is a recent grave, there isn't much to investigate that will slow down the progress on your property."

"That all makes sense. This is an old grave, from what I overheard, and it is the body of a female. If this one is from the end of the Civil War, what might an archaeologist find?"

"Clothing materials, shoes, buttons, jewelry, hair combs, and such things can date the year of death," Quincy replied. He locked eyes with Mercedes, and she knew from experience what he was not saying. The burial conditions affected evidence.

"Tammy," Mercedes said, "Please be sure Clayton and Brad know Quincy can help. I want to switch gears now and ask if this affects your feelings about the house."

Her client's exaggerated sigh whooshed through the phone speaker, then the tears followed. She said in a choked voice, "I don't know, Mercedes. I don't want to live in a haunted house, and there is so much work ahead of us. What if Sirena's spirit led you to the spot where she was so cruelly buried, and what if there are more bodies and ghosts in a basement or cellar or secret room? This is creepy and—oh, I'm sorry, this is just too much! If Clayton and I stop and put this place on the market again, will you be angry?"

"Of course not! I totally understand why you may cancel our contract," Mercedes rushed to say, watching Quincy wince and lean his head back to look heavenward. He was in the business of finding old graves. Tammy was not.

Mercedes kept her tone soothing as she said, "Talk to Clayton about it. There's no rush to let me know. But Tammy, I want to be sure you have a proper understanding about hauntings and ghosts. Sirena's spirit did not draw me to her body. Once she died in this life, she entered an eternal realm, never to return. Sirena is not hanging around, haunting people on earth until they discover and take care of her unfinished business. There are spirit beings who can, and do, interact in this world, but the Bible leaves no room for those to be the disembodied spirits of deceased human beings. I won't ask you to trust me about this. I will send you a text with the scriptures, so you'll know this for yourself."

Tammy sniffed and seemed calmer. "I'm sure you're right. I'm just used to movies and novels. Sorry I'm blubbering, I'm not myself right now. I'm hot and weary. I'll look to see what the Bible says. But that doesn't explain why people see the ghosts of soldiers on the battlefields and other strange things."

Quincy joined the conversation. "Tammy, so far, we have no reliable explanations on this side of heaven for things like that, but we can understand what they are *not*—by understanding what happens when we die. The Bible's view is what the Lord gave us. There is no in-between place here for the spirits of deceased humans to get tragically stuck in, and they don't return like Marley did to warn Scrooge in the Christmas novel. But other spiritual entities can and will deceive and confuse us about that. Have you found a church here, somewhere you can talk to your pastor?"

"Now that I hear you saying this, I know my former pastor would agree with you. Perhaps I'll call him. If we decide to stay, we will begin visiting churches, but please send me the Bible verses, if it isn't too much trouble."

"It's no trouble at all, Tammy," said Mercedes. "Unless there is something more we can do, I'm going to let you get back to Clayton and Brad. When you're ready to talk about the next steps for the house, just let me know, okay?"

"Yes. Yes, I will. Thank you ever so much, you two."

Quincy watched Mercedes put her phone in her purse and blow out a deep breath. "I'm not really in the mood to explore the cemetery now," he said solemnly.

She met his eyes and managed a weak smile. "Okay. I've lost my enthusiasm, too. There are a couple of good history museums here where we can get out of the heat. Or we can go home and decide what to do this evening."

He touched a button on his navigation system and said, "We'll return here for museums, walks, and cemeteries another time. Let's go back. Maybe we can go catch a beach breeze tonight."

They passed more of the scenic city views on the way to the South Carolina side of the Savannah River, saying little, enjoying the marshy landscape and listening to music. Quincy said, "Will you manage all right financially if this job falls through?"

"Yes. I paid my cottage rental for the entire summer, and I have the non-refundable deposit from the Popplewells and the income from the job I'm still working in Bluffton. If I finish that paperwork earlier than planned, I'll talk to a property owner there who wants to work with me. I'm emailing with a prospective client in Beaufort, but there are no signed contracts yet. I have a contract in place for the plantation house in Charleston. Attorneys have a schedule for details with the estate, and they hired me because I'm the only architectural historian who's flexible enough to work with them. I never would have gotten such an important property otherwise."

Quincy nodded slowly and looked ahead. "You'll let me know if there's anything I can do to help, right?"

They drove along under moss-laden oak branches that spanned the scenic two-lane road. She smiled and patted his arm. "Yes, I will. Thank you. Are you going to work this afternoon?"

"I didn't plan to, but as things turned out, it looks like I'll have some time. If Tammy and Clayton let Brad continue at the house, he may stumble on a basement or cellar and a wonky wall. I want to be with you if that happens, so the more I take care of this afternoon, the more time I'll have off. Do you mind?"

"Of course not! I'll work on my project as well. Do you want to drive down to the beach later?"

He grinned. "You bet. I want to make fabulous fresh memories with you, chasing the full moon as it rises tonight. My best times are with you. Bring your camera."

After sleeping in for an hour later than normal, Mercedes took breakfast out by the pool. She and Quincy spent a romantic late night enjoying a walk on the beach and a blanket in a delightful spot to watch the full moon rise over the ocean. Moon watchers crowded the beach with their cameras and relaxed under the summer night sky. For a little while, everyone was excited to watch dolphins cruising on the brilliant trail of the moon in the waves, and some speculated about whether they were the ones who swam with people lately.

She smiled at that memory when she saw her photo of the gleaming crescents of the dolphins' fins, captured with her cellphone. Munching fruit, she scrolled through all the photos and deleted duplicates. Her 'real' camera shots were better, but she needed to load those on her laptop after breakfast. She lingered over the pictures where she caught the moon through the tall dune grasses and with the luminous trail from the horizon to the surf.

Lois came out of the main house with a shiny bright pink watering can. She showered some luxurious show-stopping hibiscus flowers and waved. Mercedes wished her a good morning and motioned for her to come over to talk. "I haven't seen you much lately, and just wanted to catch up. How are things going?"

The older woman laughed. "Yes, I try to stay inside when the worst of the heat hits around here. It just saps all my energy. Aaron is helping me with some indoor projects for now. It's good to see you and Quincy are enjoying the pool. If you two want to come over sometime, I'd be glad for some company.

Aaron can't really hang around here indoors at night since the neighbors might talk. We'd welcome chaperones to watch a movie with us or play board games."

"Oh, Lois, we'd be happy to. We stay outside for the same reason, to avoid giving people the wrong impression about our relationship. But there will be evenings when it rains."

"Let's plan to get together for sure on the next rainy night," Lois said. "How is work going for you?"

When Mercedes sighed, Lois raised her brows and sat down. Mercedes told her she may have to stop her progress on the job in Savannah. "There have been some unusual and creepy things that happened this week on the property, and the owners are unsettled about everything. I sympathize with Tammy, the wife. Finding an old grave may be the last straw for her."

Lois blinked, then sat back. "That would shake anybody up! But if there's history to be learned about that house, uncovering it is a service to the community and the city. Those of us who purchase and take care of old houses, we are stewards. I'll pray the Lord's will for your clients, and that if He wants to reveal something that needs to come to light, He will give you the privilege and opportunity to join Him in the work."

Mercedes reached out to take her hand. "Thank you so much. If there is a mystery to uncover, it's good to resolve it. And if my clients choose to stick this out, I believe it will be an important step in their lives."

After breakfast and her chat with Lois, Mercedes went back to the cottage and put laundry in the washer. She loaded last night's photos into her laptop and emailed a few great ones to Quincy, some of her friends, and her parents. Then she pulled up some paperwork to finish online.

The alert on her phone told her she had a message. It was Tammy Popplewell. She reached to open the text. *Good morning, Mercedes. Can you come to the house today? Brad has found a basement door and won't open it until you are here. Isn't that weird? I mean, he's the contractor!*

Mercedes caught her breath. There was a closed-off basement!

Good morning, Tammy. I hope you are feeling better today. Does this mean you are moving ahead with plans for the house?

Clayton thinks we should let Brad give us a clean report for any potential buyer. I'm bracing myself to see what another day brings, and I'm embarrassed to be so fickle. Are you willing to stick with us for now?

Yes. I'll be there in an hour.

Next, Mercedes sent a message to Quincy to let him know she was going to Savannah to explore a long-lost basement. He said to wait on him to pick her up in ten minutes.

Chapter 6

There was no reason to dress as a professional when venturing into a basement that was sealed off for almost a hundred and sixty years. Anything Mercedes wore may never come clean. She rushed to change into a faded navy-blue cotton tee shirt and modest jean shorts and pulled her hair into a ponytail through the back of a dark-colored ball cap. Quincy had the same idea and showed up in a loose gray tee and cargo shorts. They packed a quick lunch from her refrigerator and pantry, then hurried to the Popplewell house, speculating about the kinds of things found in an Antebellum era basement that no one had been in since the Civil War.

Tammy opened the front doors for them, wiping back sweat from her forehead and trying to tidy the unruly curls that escaped from her strawberry blonde messy bun. She led them through the house to the kitchen and back door, filling them in on how the demolition work could continue and the crew clearing the overgrown yard had found a large metal cover near the foundation.

Quincy opened the door for them, and Tammy pointed to some rubble. "They left by dinner time last night. There was no evidence of a crime scene other than the body, and no reason to hold up the project any longer. I overheard there was skull damage and neck vertebrae showed strangulation. The demolition crew will be back this afternoon to haul off the debris. See those rotten old floorboards? The crew was pulling them up when they found her, so they stopped. The investigators said boards in that area got pried up and re-nailed down. Someone stuffed her under them in a shallow grave."

They stood on the patio pavers solemnly considering this news. Quincy's voice was soft when he turned to Tammy. "Thanks to you and Clayton, whoever she was, her remains will now have dignity."

Tammy nodded, then sniffed. "Yes, I suppose that's true. I read some blogs over the years about what a privilege it is to be a part of revealing and restoring history. Clayton and I thought it was about the structure and the landscaping, that the history of a house was in the records when buyers made the purchase. We thought the hard part was the remodeling process. I'm afraid I didn't come into this change in our life's direction with all I needed to face it. I doubt I have what it takes to see it through."

"Did you and Clayton pray about it?" asked Mercedes gently. "Did you have peace?"

Her client absently ran her hand over her hair again, as if tidying it. Her voice trembled. "Yes, we did. It seemed like the first opportunity to fulfill our dream of opening an inn in a place people want to visit. We like hospitality, you know, making sure people are comfortable, content, and enjoying themselves. I expected to remodel a place with character and then open it to guests, meeting people from all over. I never dreamed there would be so much darkness in a place I expected to shine with the Lord's light."

"Are you doubting Him, or yourself?" asked Quincy.

Her smile was self-conscious, and she glanced at him before looking into the rubble of the gardener's quarters. "The Lord never fails. It's me. Maybe I wanted this too much and read the lack of obstacles as a green light to go ahead." She sighed. "How does one ever know for sure? Anyway, people say He won't give us more than we can handle. But I'm questioning that, too."

Mercedes put her hand on Tammy's arm. "If you're expected to handle everything, why would you need Jesus' help at all? Why pray?"

Startled, Tammy turned to stare at her, uncomprehending. "Are you saying that's not true?"

"That's exactly what I'm saying. It's a Christian myth, like 'God helps those who help themselves.' That is not in the Bible. We need to trust Him and His strength when we have none, for that's when He shines! Jesus will faithfully go with us through the fire, as Scripture says, and not being able to do that on our own is what builds our faith. Miracles are all around us, but we call them ordinary things."

"Are you saying what I hear at church sometimes, that God will show up?"

Mercedes winced and glanced to see Quincy do the same. "No, that's another myth and one of my pet peeves is hearing church leaders say it. God is omniscient—He is everywhere, always. He is right here, right now, with you, helping you through this. That's one of His attributes. The Holy Spirit lives in born-again believers and He promised that He never leaves us. God doesn't 'show up' and 'show off,' as if He was busy somewhere else but close enough to reach us in a time of crises. His ways sometimes seem spectacular to us, but He's not so vulgar that He'd show off."

One of Brad's construction workers came around the corner with a cart loaded with cut brush and brambles. He nodded politely and said to Tammy, "You're goin' to have a whole new yard when we carry this mess away, ma'am. You can plan a beautiful garden."

"He's right, you know," said Quincy. "Look at all this light and space!"

Mercedes said, "I can envision a long veranda here with porch swings, ceiling fans, and rocking chairs, overlooking a beautiful courtyard garden your guests would love. We can browse some historic garden plans common to Savannah on my tablet if you like."

Tammy smiled now, her mood lifting. "Yes. It looks much different and will improve as we get those hedges tamed or pulled out. With the brambles being carried away from the side yards, there's an area we didn't know we had, with some garden sculpture and old pavers that are sturdy enough to move back here as part of the history of the property."

They heard Brad's voice on the left side of the house, and more men with carts of cut brush and thorny vines came around the corner. Tammy led Mercedes and Quincy in that direction, and one man warned them to beware of a huge black snake they had disturbed.

Tammy froze. Quincy stepped in front of her in his work boots, and Mercedes tagged along in old athletic shoes. She reached for Tammy's arm. "It's okay. It doesn't want to meet you, and it's good for your garden."

Reluctantly, Tammy let Mercedes lead her by the arm, scanning every step. Clayton noticed them and laughed at Tammy. Brad looked up and grinned, waving as he watched them approach.

"Glad you could make it!" he said, then directed another worker to take a full cartload of brush out of the way. He pushed his cap up and ran his hand through his hair, then settled it back on his head. "See those rotting lattice panels and those bushes we dug up? They were there to hide an ugly box structure, here," he announced, pointing to bricks and a large, rusted metal panel near to the ground. "Maybe someone assumed it was an old well that was dangerous, so they landscaped around it. But I believe this metal lays over an opening to a basement or cellar. I just need to figure out how to raise it. There's no handle or lock."

Quincy squatted next to the bricks and ran a finger over crumbling masonry. "If the Popplewells give us permission, we can remove these bricks and see what's under the metal. This must come down anyway. It's a hazard."

He and Brad looked at Clayton, who nodded and said, "What can I do to help?"

"You can bring me those tools in that belt bag," answered Brad. He looked at Quincy. "Grab a pair of those safety glasses over there."

Two of his men with empty carts appeared around the corner, and he called them to help. Quincy stood back, and Brad asked him to use his phone to snap some photos of the structure before and during the process.

Tammy stayed by Mercedes' side, out of range of any flying chips from the chisels loosening the masonry. When the construction crew pulled a section of the bricks away, Brad found that the corroded metal piece rested in a framework that was easily pushed out from the inside, and one of his men quickly inserted a crowbar into the gap, lifting it off.

"Well, that's a first for me," Brad said. "They made the cover for coming out, not for going in."

Quincy took photos of what was under the cover, and Mercedes took a few steps that direction. But Tammy stood rooted where she was. Clayton looked up and extended his hand to her, so she walked over to be at his side. "It's okay, there's nothing but crude stairs, made of rock."

The odor of damp wood and stone rose from the dark hole, and they all stared down at where the steps ended. "Could be worse," announced Brad. "The ventilation grills around the foundation let the room breathe all these years, but that means it suffers from the humidity, as well. I'll see if the structure is safe from a cave-in."

He left the sweltering, sunlit day to descend into the unknown. Mercedes started praying silently for his safety and saw Quincy squirm, itching to go into the murky space. Soon, Brad called one of his men for a few of the loose bricks, and they shored up an area of shelving on the verge of tumbling down. Then the other man came out coughing, brushing off spider webs and dust.

Brad appeared at the bottom step, coughing, before he asked Clayton if Quincy could come down first and take some photos of the basement. Clayton nodded and Quincy smiled at Mercedes before descending.

They heard muffled voices while Brad and Quincy examined and recorded the safety of the underground structure. Two of Brad's men went on with the work of carting off the undergrowth and lawn waste. Then Quincy came to the bottom step and called up for Mercedes.

She rushed to the opening and looked down while he told her the supporting structure was sound. He asked her to come in with her tablet for the photos she would need for her records. Fine particles of dust rose from the hole like a soft mist, but she pulled the device out of her bag and turned it on, then took her first cautious steps down. Her instinct was to put her free hand on the block wall in case she lost her balance, or a hewn stone step gave way, but a first look told her she would only touch those spider-webbed walls in the direst of emergencies. Even as she took the next step, a startled roach scurried into a dark crevice. She shivered, and above her, Tammy must have been watching. She yelped.

Mercedes reached the bottom as Tammy was telling Clayton she would never go down there, not even if they found gold and diamonds. But as her eyes adjusted to the shadowy shapes around her, Mercedes gasped. Quincy turned and grinned, excitement lighting up his face. "Brad tells me this could be the only discovery of its kind left in the South."

"Contraband and blockade runner goods!" Mercedes was incredulous. She stood in disbelief, staring at crates, boxes, and packed shelves.

Quincy jerked his head to point back at her. "She knows far more than I do about American history, and she grew up in Charleston."

Brad wiped dust from the stenciled lettering on a wooden crate and whistled. "If this really is what it says it is, whatever you do, don't light a match down here. We'll get blown sky high."

Mercedes came closer. "That's what happened the night Columbia, South Carolina, burned to the ground when the

Union troops went through. It was all built of wood, a kindling box. I read in a Union soldier's diary of that night that basements stocked with weapons and ammunition exploded in one house and then another when they caught fire. The Union soldier wrote about how amazed he was they packed so many houses with weapon stores. He was gleeful, of course, saying South Carolina got what they deserved for seceding from the United States." She dusted off another crate label. "But that's not what happened here, guys. The owners abandoned this place to the war. If Granny's story is true, I believe Jack Haute, the carpetbagger who moved in, scavenged, and stole items from around Savannah when the Union occupied it. He was selling them from the house."

Quincy examined another crate, squinting to focus on the lettering. "Makes sense to me. My expertise is not in American historic events or collections, but I've heard food became scarce in the South because of the Northern blockades. This crate seems to be packed with cupboard tins of food."

"This one has sewing supplies. I believe Miss Ellison is right. These seem to be stocked for resale or barter, not a family pantry," said Brad.

Mercedes had her tablet up, taking photos of the basement and inventory. She said, "Well, whatever someone stored here came in after they opened the metal door another way, from inside the house. I think the flash on my tablet camera has revealed at least one door. We should get some lights in here and look."

Her ear tickled with Quincy's warm breath, sending a delightful shiver down her neck in the dim light. "That's my girl," he whispered.

After a break for lunch, Mercedes, Quincy, and Brad gathered some flashlights to explore the basement while the construction crew helped load up the rubble from the demolished gardener's quarters. Brad had a number to call a historic society about their discovery, but knew it was going to cause a lot of attention and set the remodeling project back. He wanted to find an entrance first and work from inside the house.

He led the way again as they took the stone steps in hard hats, safety glasses, and work gloves, carrying large flashlights. Brad and Quincy wore tool belts, and Brad used a tape measure to estimate how far into the house foundation the basement went. Mercedes suggested they try pulling away the cover that blocked one window to let in more light. Crates and boxes obstructed the other windows. But when Brad pried away an old board from the small opening, the glass was too filthy to allow much light in the room.

A wooden wall jutted out to block the view of a door Mercedes saw in her photos before lunch. Quincy found it, and stairs in an alcove behind it led to the door. He and Brad navigated the hazards of the rotting wood and tried to force the door open. But it was nailed shut on the other side.

Frustrated, Brad looked at Mercedes. "I have a drill in a case outside those stone steps. Can you bring it down? Maybe we can make a hole in the door or the wall and look for it inside the house."

She left to get the drill, and Brad stood on his perch at the top step in front of the door, scanning the basement. He caught his breath and tapped Quincy on the shoulder. "There's a ladder over there. Maybe it's only propped up, but I believe it's attached with brackets to the block wall by a trap door. It's hard to see from the floor, but will you check it out?"

Quincy moved in that direction, peeking behind crates and shelving. Mercedes arrived with the drill, and Brad set to work on penetrating the door and wood framing. By the time he finished, Quincy and Mercedes had spied the old ladder behind boxes labeled as tea and coffee.

"I can't bring in a ladder that will let me lean over that far, and it's too dangerous to climb on those rotted crates," Brad announced. "If we can move them aside just enough, I'll slide through and find out what's going on back there. Let's try it."

Once he was through, Mercedes and Quincy waited expectantly for Brad's assessment of the ladder and its destination, keeping their flashlight beams at the trapdoor. But Brad told them they could lower them for now, because after squeezing behind the inventory, there was enough space built under the shelves for a hidden hallway of sorts. He followed the end of it and popped out near the stone stairway out of the basement, announcing he was going up to get a ladder to reach the drop-down door in the ceiling.

"What? Is it safe?" squeaked Mercedes.

Beside her, Quincy said sternly, "No, not for you. Your mama would kill me if I let you go back there. Stay here."

"Quincy," she said, grabbing his arm. "Please, be careful. These walls and the framework look solid, but those shelves may not be. Think of the weight they've supported for over fifteen decades."

Alone in the dim light, he grinned and pulled her close, rubbing her back. She turned her head to avoid hitting his chin with the bill of her hard hat, but he reached up to remove it. "Like old times, huh? You never liked it when I went into risky places."

"Don't let anything bad happen to you," she whispered.

He leaned closer and planted a lingering kiss on her temple. She whispered, "Yes, this is certainly like old times. You knew then that this would distract me."

There was a bang of metal on stone as Brad pointed his ladder down the entrance steps. With a rogue's smile, Quincy settled her hard hat on her head again. Brad called to him at the tunnel opening to help maneuver the ladder into it, and he had to accept Quincy's help to get it through to the ceiling door.

Mercedes prayed they would be safe and ran her eyes over items on the top shelves. To her relief, all were lightweight. But it seemed to take forever before the men pulled the ladder up to the door and tried in vain to push through it. Brad asked Mercedes to hand the drill through the shelving to Quincy, who handed it up to him. As he did with the old door at the top of the shelves, Brad made some drill holes through the walls to look for inside the house.

When they came out from the shelving tunnel with the ladder, they all left the close atmosphere of the basement and came up for fresh air in the side yard, which was now clear of brambles and vines.

Chapter 7

Aaron ducked into Lois' patio door with a platter of grilled hamburgers and hot dogs in the nick of time. The rain from a summer storm poured so hard it roared on the roof and made it hard to see anything out the windows, and Lois wondered aloud if it would damage her flowers.

Mercedes and Quincy told the older couple some of the day's events as they put out the last of the items for a burger bar on the kitchen island, where they spread out a crock pot full of chili, a bowl of coleslaw, chopped onions, dill pickle relish, and every topping they could think of. Quincy claimed to be ravenous after all the work they did in Savannah, and Aaron said the coming storm meant he had to plan an early supper from the grill. So, they made a date for a dinner and movie night.

No one said much after Aaron blessed the meal and they began eating. They heaped the burgers too tall to fit into a normal mouth, and Mercedes giggled at Quincy's attempt to make it work, anyway. But she was hungry, too, and finished a loaded burger, slaw, and potato chips. Aaron and Lois contributed something to conversation now and then, but it was only when they brought out the fresh strawberries from the day's shopping at the Farmer's Market in Bluffton that Quincy and Mercedes slowed down enough to talk about what they found in the basement in Savannah.

Aaron was especially interested and asked questions from a contractor's point of view. Then he asked if they knew when Brad would search for the drilled holes to find the doors.

Quincy swallowed his last bite of strawberries and coconut cream and patted his mouth with his napkin. "He hopes to do that tomorrow, but he's also working with the city's historical societies to evaluate the contents of the basement. The ammunition and gunpowder for those weapons stored there could mean we can't work inside the house at all until they remove the fire hazard. So, we'll wait on Tammy to let Mercedes know when we can go back."

"And in the meantime, this alters my paperwork on the property," added Mercedes. "I'm in a whole new sphere of records and reporting, updating the listing on the house and registering it with more historical sites. If my clients decide to move forward and keep me under contract, I will be in new territory with my experience."

Reaching for her hand, Quincy laughed. "You took this job hoping it would be monotonous and easy."

She laughed, too. "So much for my careful plan to enjoy a relaxing summer of boring paperwork by day and beach, biking, swimming, and kayaking by night and weekends."

Aaron chuckled as he set down his glass of iced tea. He looked over at Lois. "We know about how sideways plans can go with remodeling and restoration, don't we, Lois?"

"Yes, we do. There's always something unexpected, and I'm glad I knew a good contractor with time on his hands," she said, smiling back at Aaron. "But I admit, I've never been in a situation like the couple in Savannah. They haven't even made it to what I thought was the hardest part of restoration."

Mercedes met Quincy's eyes and then turned back to Lois. "Tammy is questioning whether they misunderstood God. None of this was part of their dream for a place to open an inn. She wonders if the all the darkness they have encountered invalidates the house as being a place she intended for sharing light."

Lois reached over to pat her hand. "I am praying for her, and for you and Quincy as you try to help. Light drives away the darkness, and we can pray over the property."

Aaron reached for Quincy and Lois' hands and asked them all to join him in praying for Mercedes' clients and the property they hoped to use in service to the Lord. They each shared their heart about the situation, but asked Jesus to bring about His will and His best for everyone concerned.

After clearing away dinner, they streamed an old movie on the television screen together while the storm rolled in and out like a tide over Bluffton. Aaron left during a lull in the thunder and lightning.

The rain had stopped, and Mercedes walked Quincy out to his car, which he parked behind her Jeep so neighbors could see Aaron was not alone with Lois.

"I really, really enjoyed spending today with you," he said, swinging their clasped hands.

She grinned and looked up at him. "You were in your element, being Indiana Jones again. I think that was your favorite part."

He threw his head back and laughed. "Okay, it was close, but you know my favorite part is when I'm doing anything or nothing by your side. We work well together. Why don't I come over in the morning before it gets too hot outside, say, eight o'clock? We'll take our laptops on the lounge chairs by the pool for a couple of hours of work. Who knows, Tammy may text us about progress in the house, and if not, we'll see where we're at in our schedules. Maybe we can call it a day at lunchtime, and you can help me go get groceries."

"I'd love that."

A light mist fell again. Thunder rumbled in the distance as she kissed his cheek, and he kissed her forehead. "Goodnight, beautiful. Try to dream about me," he said in a husky voice, his lips brushing her forehead.

She smiled and murmured, "That would be delicious, at the top of my list. I'll try."

Mercedes slipped under the soft sheets shortly after returning to her cottage. The storm's intensity had increased, making the windows flash often. On the nightstand beside her bed, the little stuffed pocket toy of Bijou that Quincy had given her kept a watch.

She intended to sleep, but she noticed her Great-Great Grand Aunt's journal where it laid on her dresser with a stack of other books. It reminded her of the antique cedar chest and the cleverly hidden panel built into it to conceal the journal and important deeds and papers. People in times past seemed to be more creative about hiding things, like the basement found at the Popplewell house earlier that day. The way out of it was not the way into it, and previous owners were unaware of it. Even the dastardly way a woman's body was hidden under the floor of the unoccupied gardener's quarters was so successful that only time and ruin for the building revealed her burial.

The story Tonya's grandmother passed along from generations in her family was told from the gardener's perspective, and he was a relative. If Granny's account was reliable, blood connected her family with the servants who got sent on their way when the builders of the main house had to abandon it. What kind of man was Sirena's brother? Tonya's grandmother said he was unhappy with his sister being used as the mistress of the carpetbagger. Could he have confronted her as she tried to sneak out for a night spent in the main house with Jack Haute? Could the gardener have accidentally killed his sister and buried her under the floor, then made up the story of hearing her confront her lover and another mistress, trying to get revenge on Haute by blaming him for her disappearance? Was there any record of him going for help and to law enforcement that night, as Granny's account claimed?

Another boom of thunder and strobe-light flashes outside her window made the lamp go off. She turned the switch so it wouldn't come on during the night when the power came back, then she snuggled down into the soft sheets. But her mind was still mulling over the mysteries of the Popplewell house. One thing Granny was right about was that the carpetbagger who took over the main house was serious about making money. The stash of goods in the basement did not come cheap back then. If he was the scam artist, thief, and swindler they said he was, it would not surprise Mercedes. He would not have walked away from that kind of profit, either. Something happened to him before he could sell everything off. Was his activity so illegal that he kept no records, or did he hide the receipts as blackmail against being caught? In such a case, he had leverage over everyone implicated in his business. Sirena's brother was probably only one of many citizens in Savannah who would murder him.

As she yawned and turned over to go to sleep, Mercedes prayed that if there was any justice to be satisfied or any beneficial history in the Popplewell house that should come to light, Jesus would bring it into the open—with or without her working for Tammy and Clayton.

Quincy sat on a shaded poolside lounge chair near Mercedes, sipping the lemon tea she brought out with breakfast. He scowled at the screen of his laptop.

"Why such a fierce face?" she asked, bemused.

His smile was fleeting. "You're supposed to be concentrating on super-detail-oriented paperwork that would drive most people out of their minds," he quipped, turning his eyes back to the screen.

"I had to take a break from the details before I lost my mind," she teased. "About every thirty minutes in front of a computer screen, we're supposed to get up and walk around for three minutes, you know. That's the current wisdom, though I've been doing that for as long as I can remember. That's the secret to having this super-power of mine, as well as using soft background music to keep my pacing steady."

He glanced up and smiled distractedly. She said his name, so he looked up again.

"What are you working on?"

"Oh—I finished with one contact and checked progress on my part in the Lenoir Bassett and Madigan investigation a few weeks ago. The case is solid. He won't get out of it without serving time, and the other two are likely to meet a similar fate. But I can't share more details with you. Confidentially and ongoing legal stuff, you know."

"Oh. So, you hide things from me."

Startled, his head jerked up. He was tongue-tied for a few moments. "That's not it at all! I really am limited about what I can reveal at certain times, you know that. It's just more difficult because—well, you're part of it, yet not part of it."

"Yeah. It's okay. I'll go back to my mind-numbing online forms now."

She sighed and started touching her laptop screen to move pages and then typed with lightning speed. Quincy watched from the corner of his eye, feeling guilty. What he saw on his laptop made him feel fierce, as she said, and it was nothing he could tell her. But if he were in her place, he would want to know that Stanley Lenoir's son was jealous of Zach Boone's link to his family and the papers that were found to make him a partner with the firm. If they convicted his father of anything in the coming months, he vowed vengeance for what he claimed was a conspiracy with Zach, Mercedes, Jana, and Declan. How he would explain the attempted murder of Mercedes by his father's bodyguards was anyone's guess.

He closed the tab on the screen and then shut his laptop altogether. With a sigh and an exaggerated move to stretch his arms, he turned to look at her. "I can't get any work done, anyway, with such a beautiful view."

She rolled her eyes and kept typing. "Oh, yeah? Are you going back to your place, then?"

He got up from the chair and leisurely made his way behind her, then massaged her shoulders. "No, I think I'll just throw you into the pool instead. Then we'll both have a break from work at the same time."

"Ah, well, I don't think so. I'm not dressed for a swim."

"That makes it more interesting. Okay, how about a slow dance? Find a song on your phone."

Mercedes stopped typing and sighed. He took her laptop from her and set it on a table, then picked up her phone from its spot on the same table. It vibrated in his hand and made a soothing notification sound. Startled, he looked down and saw a name and a photo scroll across the screen for a text message. *Zach.*

She groaned at the sound of the notification behind her and held out her hand. He walked up and passed the phone to her. "Maybe it's Tammy," she said.

Quincy was silent and watched while she opened the phone with her password and checked to see who the message was from. Instead of looking at it, she flicked impatiently to the next screen and found her favorite music app. She chose a romantic 1980s song she knew he liked and stood up, sliding her arms luxuriously around him for a slow dance.

He thrilled to her touch and tried to shake off the unpleasant surprise in his mind. It was time to enjoy a break from work to be with her. One of his favorite things was to hold her and slow dance, for it melted away all her distractions and kept her focus on him. Besides, Mercedes made a brutal point a while ago about him keeping secrets, so she would not keep any from him.

She was hiding nothing from him about Zach, he told himself again. But he was hiding something significant from her, and it was about Zach. And he wanted to know what Zach had to say about anything at all.

Tammy did not send a message, and something distracted Mercedes all afternoon. Quincy asked her to go out to lunch and to shop for groceries with him. While they were out, a new gluten-free product in the grocery store prompted her to mention a funny conversation with her friend Jana, and he asked if Jana and her boyfriend Declan ever saw Zach.

Mercedes shrugged and an edge of irritation crept into her voice. "Jana said they saw him show up at church last week and they went to sit with him. He and Declan text and call each other sometimes, sharing job application information. They both have some prospects. I suppose he's doing well."

Quincy nodded. "Good. But you still haven't heard from him about that night? He never asked if they hurt you?"

"No. This morning, I got the first text since that day, but I don't know if I'll open it."

They were in the frozen foods section, and she chose a non-dairy cashew milk ice cream in a velvety dark chocolate truffle flavor. "Yum," he said. "Get two of those. So, about Zach, is it true there's a thin line between love and hate?"

A smile replaced her annoyance, and she glanced at him through the clear spot on the fogging glass door of the frozen fruit section. "No, silly! We only dated in person about seven or eight times, though Jana said he rarely sees a girl more than twice. I liked and admired him, that's all, and he never said how he felt about me. He told the firm we were in a serious relationship and hinted to me that something was 'next' for us after he had a job, as if I could read his mind. Zach's a slippery fish in dating relationships. It would never occur to him I didn't want him because women always did. That night, on the beach with Jana and Declan, I said it was time to call our undefined relationship over. He shook it off as totally unserious."

Quincy mulled over this revelation about her relationship with Zach as he followed her, pushing the grocery cart. He watched them that night as he did surveillance for the agency, snagging Stanley Lenoir, and he was jealous of how Zach's suave confidence conveyed commitment to her.

She said little else except to discuss their food choices. When they got to the cottage, he helped carry her bags in, then asked, "What's bothering you, Mercedes? You're not yourself today."

Setting her mesh market bag full of produce on the countertop, she sighed and pushed back her hair with her hands. "I really want to know what's going on at the Popplewell house in Savannah. I thought through a lot of scenarios last night about how Tonya's Granny's story might have happened. There's an unsolved mystery there, and I hope to be part of bringing it to light. Tammy and Clayton may stop the restoration and sell the house, ending my chance to know what happened so long ago."

Quincy wanted to shout with relief that her mind was on the Popplewell property instead of her recent breakup. He reached for her and wrapped her in a hug. It will work out right. Listen to some music, take a nap, and get things done around the cottage until this evening. Want to ride bikes somewhere?"

Mercedes nodded against his shoulder. "Okay. Let's ride to a little beach Lois told me about on the river and watch the sunset."

Armies of tiny fiddler crabs marched at random over mudflats and bubbles rose from burrows of mollusks on the sandy riverside as Mercedes and Quincy explored Alljoy Beach. Acres of spartina grass sprouted up across the May River, and kayakers floated along the same waters as cruising dolphins.

"What's that snap, crackle, and pop sound?" asked Quincy, screening his sunglasses with his hand.

Mercedes laughed and pointed. "Barnacles. You can hear them better from underwater, but the important thing is that you can hear them at all. This is off the beaten path, a last frontier, according to Lois. It's the only place left that feels like Old Bluffton did before marketers rebranded it. She said businesses closed every Wednesday afternoon because people went down to enjoy the river."

Above them, a river breeze rattled palmetto fronds. Quincy turned to look at tin roofs of cottages standing behind elephant ears and banana trees. "It's a quirky, mellow, organic place," he noted.

A handful of trucks with hitches and boat trailers parked in the boat access area, and two senior citizens with a lap dog parked there in a golf cart, watching the activity on the river. Nearby, a woman in a bathing suit top and shorts read a cheap paperback in her lawn chair.

"Let's go to park under that big oak and walk around," Mercedes suggested. They rode their cruiser bikes to the shade, propping them on the kickstands while tiny green lizards on the tree bark scampered away.

Someone with a cast net in the river shouted he caught a shark, and friends came up around him to see, knee deep in the salty water. Quincy glanced at Mercedes in alarm. She laughed and said, "It's a swimming area. If they catch a shark, it will be small, not the kind that can eat you. He may have a stingray on the net, too. When you walk into the river, shuffle your feet a little along the bottom. The rays will go away."

They came to a concrete bench with ecological graffiti messages and paintings about saving sea turtles, and Mercedes pulled his arm to sit down with her. "On Hilton Head and in this area, slaves and servants had a list of things to do during the day, and after that, they were free to farm, fish, and otherwise provide for themselves or relax. Sometimes they used cast nets, like the one the boy out there caught the baby shark in. Fish, shrimp, oysters, and other food were plentiful."

He drew a deep breath of the salty river breeze. "It's so peaceful here. So unassuming. Maybe we can come back with kayaks, or I can read while you paint the view from your easel."

"I'd love that. Look, over there, soon the sun will set over the river, like the night we watched from the Calhoun Street Pier. I'm going to take some photos this time. Can I get one of you?"

He grinned. "Of course!"

The sky was changing, and several joggers paused, panting, under the shade tree near the bicycles, to watch the sunset. A car with a courting couple parked to await the coming darkness.

Mercedes took a few photos of Quincy—on the bench with the oak tree and moss, one with the palms, and one with the river behind him. Soft, flattering colors of a coming sunset tinted his face. A teen walking by offered to snap their portrait together with her phone camera. He beamed as he showed them the screen and told them how great it would look on social media.

Mercedes smiled and reached for her phone. "We're not on social media, but we have websites and blogs we can use it on. This is a special photo and we're so grateful. Thank you!"

Standing by the riverside on the sandy beach, Mercedes and Quincy stood watching the colorful pageant of another romantic sunset. It unfolded lazily, like most things do in the Lowcountry. There was no reason to rush, no better view and no better place to be. Quincy slid his arm around her shoulders, and she slid hers around his waist. Just as the last light of the sun flashed on the horizon, he leaned over and kissed her temple. "You know that girl or guy people see in the movies when time slows down? That's who you are to me. I love you," he murmured.

Mercedes smiled and hugged him. She tiptoed and said near his ear, "I love you, too. Alljoy Beach is a wonderful name for a place to promise my love to you again."

Chapter 8

Saturday morning started out with a long to-do list for Mercedes at her cottage. Though she was still in after-glow from the evening with Quincy at Alljoy Beach, she needed to let her feet touch the ground. Her schedule had been disrupted by the twists and turns with her job in Savannah, which she may or may not get to complete. She had laundry and ironing to do, some meal planning and cooking ahead to accomplish, and her family and friends were waiting on responses to texts, emails, and phone calls.

Including Zach. She had not opened his.

Upbeat oldies music helped her get chores done faster, so she started out with that for the mundane checklist. But lyrics bothered her when she was working or responding to texts and email, so she switched to epic music soundtracks before sitting down with her phone and a salad for lunch. It was easy to catch up with her mom, brother, and best friends in Charleston. She took more time with her Bible Study group text, noting prayer requests in her prayer journal. As she was scrolling, a new message came in from Jana, who said Zach told Declan she was not responding to his text.

Mercedes sighed. Zach would have to be dealt with, or it would look bad to Jana and Declan—which may be intentional on his part. After all, he told her worst enemy in the world and their mutual friend Declan that she was the worst thing that ever happened to him; she ruined his life, and he never wanted to see her again.

She quickly texted Jana. *I saw his text but can't imagine what more he can say to me or about me. Unless it's an apology, please tell him to move on.*

Jana sent a message back. *I wish I knew what he was texting you about. He didn't tell Declan, who is going nuts wanting to know. And I admit I'm curious. I mean, the guy is one cool customer with women. He was adamant and downright mean about what he thought of you when he talked to Declan that night when he fled Hilton Head in a rented car. Maybe he's been praying about it and regrets what he said and did? It could be an apology, but I wouldn't blame you if you didn't open it and blocked his number. It's up to you.*

Mercedes posted an emoticon rolling its eyes. *I'll let you know if I open it.*

Then, a message came in from Tammy. *Hi, Mercedes. The historic society group is still working with removal of the museum finds from the basement. They made us leave yesterday in case there was any danger, but that's clear now. Brad asked to come by this morning to look for the doors he drilled holes around, but he can't find them anywhere in the house. He wants to try again on Monday with a demolition crew on hand and asked if you will please be here. He would like Quincy to come if he can. Around nine thirty on Monday morning?*

Mercedes' heart rate shot up, and she stood to her feet by the kitchen table. *I will be there! I'm sure Quincy will clear his schedule to be available as well.*

Good, I will tell Brad. And Clayton and I will visit a local church tomorrow morning. I appreciate your patience with me last week. You set me to thinking about a lot of things.

Smiling a little, Mercedes responded. *I'm honored if anything I said helped.* Then she added a heart emoticon.

Next, she sent Quincy a text. *Hi, handsome. Thought you might want to know I accepted a date with Brad. He wants to meet at the Popplewell house on Monday morning at nine thirty—with a demolition crew! He'd like for you to come too.*

She cleared away her dishes while she waited for Quincy to respond, then pulled out a muffin pan for some baking to have for busy days the next week. His message popped back, and she rushed over to reach for her phone.

Nice of Mr. Power by the Hour to invite me. Maybe he knows I'm the jealous type. And I'm excited to hear we're finally knocking down some walls! Is this because he can't find the holes he drilled?

That's right.

I guessed as much, and he probably expected it. There was no light coming through them. Listen, I got an invitation from a group of my friends around the globe to get together for another Bible study in the morning. My landlords will be a couple hours away representing the Gideons at a church, and we visited with Lois and Aaron in theirs last week. Will it work out for you to be in the video session with me to do the study with my friends? The topic this week is Colossians 1:15-20, about who Jesus is.

Mercedes selected a happy emoticon face to begin her response. *That sounds fantastic! Love to see the old gang again and meet any fresh faces. I'll write the verses down and prepare after I get my chores done. Looking forward to fun with you later.*

It was a couple of hours before Mercedes sat down, ready to check off the last thing on her list. Her heart fluttered as her finger hovered over Zach's name. There was a time when she hoped to hear from him. Now, seeing his picture and his name annoyed her.

A deep breath and a touch of her finger sent her across the line into his territory. She blinked at his message. *I miss you. I wish things were different.*

"What?" she exclaimed to the empty living room of her cottage. "Really?"

In her mind, she went back to that last night with him in Hilton Head, when he said the romantic ocean view they shared on the beach was so perfect. Then he added he wished things were different. He never explained his statement, and she assumed it was because they had escaped from the company cookout and the menacing presence of Stanley Lenoir. Now, "different" could mean many things, and none of them appealed to her.

She sent her response. *Oh, yeah? Says the guy who declares I'm the worst thing that ever happened to him, that I ruined his life, and he never wants to see me again. Save it, Zach. Things aren't different. They are what they are, and you made yourself crystal clear. Men attacked me and left me for dead because of your selfish ambition, and you ran out of town in a fury without even checking to see if I was okay. I honestly, sincerely hope you will get all the good things you've been working so hard for in life. I'm not on that list, and I've moved on.*

On Monday morning, Quincy and Mercedes arrived at the Popplewell property in Savannah with anticipation. They were uncertain what the day would bring, but they doubted it would be boring.

Brad and Clayton updated them on the status of items being removed from the basement while Tammy made tea and coffee for everyone. No one was certain which experts in which cities would evaluate the artifacts, or when they might get displayed, or sold, into collections.

"All we can be certain about is that no one is certain," quipped Brad, who rolled his eyes. "But I'm satisfied that I can now move ahead to work for Clayton and Tammy."

Clayton sighed and turned with a furtive glance at the kitchen door. "We can proceed for now. Tammy is feeling better after a weekend of rest and attending a worship service yesterday. We're both grateful to have been the owners during the important historical find in the unknown basement, and I'm encouraged that our real estate agent said she could have made so much more on the sale, if only this discovery was part of the house's history. So, Tammy knows we can stop, sell for a profit, and find a more boring property. We want to know if there's anything else in the house and frankly, I want to solve the mystery of a possible hidden room and doors—without stumbling on any more bodies."

Tammy came out of the kitchen wearing an apron and a warm smile, balancing a tray of steaming cups, teaspoons, honey, and sugar. "Sorry, no cream, if anyone wanted it. What about your demolition crew, Brad? Will they be wanting anything?"

Brad waited for the others to take a cup and picked up one full of coffee. "No ma'am, they will have a thermos. Thank you for this, though. They got delayed and should be here in half an hour. There's no reason we can't start lookin' around."

Mercedes and Quincy added honey to their tea and Mercedes asked Tammy if she needed help in the kitchen. But her host waved her off with a chuckle. "Oh, no, sweet friend, you should be off doing what you do best while I do what I do best. Spiritual gifts, you know. That's what the sermon was about yesterday."

She went to turn on a large box fan that would blow into the interior of the house through the looming shadows in the hallway. Quincy winked at Mercedes over his cup, and they turned to listen to Brad as he answered questions for Clayton. Yes, if he could determine the most likely place for the doors based on measurements in the basement, he may tear down lath and plaster walls and shiplap. The wiring on the house needed a makeover, so they would update plaster with drywall. He would salvage as much as possible to be used in future décor.

"The split staircase is the heart of the house," Brad drawled, narrowing his brown eyes and tilting his head in concentration. "I want to bang around under the side that leads to the second floor."

Clayton picked up a chunk of plaster that fell from the wall over the weekend, examining the new spiderweb of cracks around the exposed wood lath material. "It's coming down anyway," he said.

"Yes, it is. Even the areas where previous owners replaced the plaster with drywall are now out of date with building codes. For safety reasons, this will come out."

They heard voices as Tammy welcomed the rest of the construction crew. She led them to Brad and then loaded the empty cups into her tray to return to the kitchen.

Mercedes, Quincy, and Clayton stepped back out of the way, and Mercedes pulled out her tablet to have the property records and notes available. Brad's team explored around the most likely location for the height of a door and found his drill hole under some plaster that easily crumbled away. After measurements and some cuts with a saw, they uncovered a sealed wooden door with no trim covered in lath and plaster.

"Why would anyone cover this up?" puzzled Clayton. "It's the easy way down."

"To hide something, in this case," said Mercedes. "Brad, can you explore the short wall under the landing? That's five feet of wasted space that people would build storage into."

Brad directed his men where she pointed, and when they cut through, they found a small opening with the door trim removed. The worker who revealed it turned to Brad. "It's sealed, too. I can't open it from here."

"Every time we walk upstairs, I catch a whiff of tobacco," said Mercedes. "It is on my list of recommendations for the Popplewells to find the source and eliminate it if they are opening an inn. I assumed it had permeated the varnish, wallpaper, and paint, but now that we uncovered all the goods in the basement, I have an idea. Can we see if there's an opening to this storage area on the landing?"

Brad's brows had shot up when she was talking. Now his eyes sparked with possibilities. He went up the steps to the turn in the staircase on a large landing. Another construction worker followed him up, curious. They didn't see an opening in the hardwood floor but detected that there was no caulking, filler, or shoe molding trim around the flooring and posts.

"Why not lift the floor?" suggested Quincy with a shrug.

Brad muttered, "Why not, indeed!" He got his fellow worker to help him pull up on the lip, overhanging the landing to the first step. The floor squawked in protest but came up rather easily. A metal prop along the side held it up.

Clayton gasped and stood staring, open-mouthed. The smell of blended tobacco rose from the hole. Brad looked down in disbelief and whistled, then summoned Clayton with his hand.

Hesitantly, uncertain of whether he wanted to know what Brad found, Clayton took the creaking old steps up to stand close enough to see. "My word," he breathed. "Look at those funny old tobacco tins. Is that box labeled as clay pipes?"

"You bet it is! And I see another one for tins of chewing tobacco and snuff," said Brad, pointing. "Take photos with your camera and get Tammy to come in here."

"I'll get her!" cried Mercedes, and she ran down the hallway to the kitchen, calling for Tammy. By the time the ladies returned, Clayton and Brad had moved boxes and discovered Brad's drill holes and the drop-down door opening to the ladder in the basement.

Chapter 9

They lay the floor opening back down after a half hour of exploring the cache of tobacco products. Tammy expressed her relief that there were no burials under the stairs and that there was nothing sinister about the two sealed doors along the side of the upper stairs. She and Clayton must decide whether to restore the house to the original plan with a replacement door and stairs down to the basement or choose to drywall over the doors again and create an entry from outside.

Next, Brad wanted to tackle the mystery of the square footage measurements on the second floor. As they took the stairs, Mercedes asked him his opinion about why there was an odd cut-out section where they could see the downstairs hallway from the ornate wooden stair and landing railings. The railing ended at a point where the floor and plaster wall of the next floor began, and they were using handrails secured to that section of the plaster wall. Since there was an open hallway on the first floor where they found the basement door, she thought there should have been an open hallway on the second floor, with a safety railing like the staircase interior section had. This would have allowed light from a window to fall on the stairs and hallways and allowed better air circulation.

"The handrail on the plaster going upstairs doesn't match either the inner railing design or the handrail on the first floor," she pointed out. "Someone could have added later because of the failure of the original one, but the architect who designed this house would not have built that cut-out to the hall below. He obviously meant the staircase to be impressive as guests arrived in the grand entryway. It was a showpiece in the home's heart, not something boxed in like this. It just makes little sense."

The men looked things over and agreed with her. One of the workmen started using a tape measure and then went down to the hall below. He came back and announced that the area of the hallway beside the stairs on the first floor was exactly the space added to the rooms on that side of the second floor.

"So, there could have been a hallway, and someone enclosed it. Maybe for closet space?" pondered Brad.

Quincy walked into the room at the end of the hall. "The two bedrooms in the hall on the first floor opened to the hall beside the stairs. Instead, this bedroom opens to the middle hallway, and the next room opens into this one, not a hallway. Neither has a closet to account for that space by the stairs."

One of Brad's men leaned in to say something to him. Brad nodded and looked at Clayton and the crew headed downstairs. "My crew is due for a lunch break now. We can eat something, too, or keep looking around for half an hour until they come back in."

"I'm too keyed up to eat," said Clayton, and the others laughed.

"We're staying here to explore," said Quincy with a look at Mercedes. She nodded.

"Good!" said Brad. "I can't rest until we solve another mystery. Quincy and Mercedes, you take the far corner room, and Clayton, you look this hallway over. I'll take the first room. We're looking for telltale signs of joins in plaster. Thump on the walls to listen for hollow and solid space."

Mercedes and Quincy went into the first bedroom, so they could get to the door for the second bedroom at the far back corner of the house. It was an odd arrangement, but not unheard of. Governesses, nannies, and other caregivers could have used the room next to a child's room. Servants could have shared adjoining rooms, and one room may have served as a sitting room from a bedroom.

She went to the grimy windows that overlooked the backyard space. From them, there was a view past the rickety locked gate into a narrow strip that looked like a utility or common space that backed up to a yard bursting with colorful hydrangeas and other flowers.

Then her heart jumped. A woman with gray hair and a kindly face stood up straight with her watering can and looked directly into the window at her. Her face was solemn. With a sad smile, she nodded. *Granny*, Mercedes thought, and she pressed her hand to the glass and smiled back.

She turned to Quincy's voice in the room. "The inner wall is the only potential link to the enclosed hallway space," he said, standing with hands on hips, staring at scarred old built-in bookcases. "There's no plaster to thump on."

Mercedes sighed and rolled her eyes. "I hope we don't find a moving bookcase. What a cliché!"

He chuckled, running his hands over decades of sticky film and dusty scratches on sections of wood. "There's a reason the moving bookcases and fireplace mantles show up in stories, you know. We'll rule out this wall of them and hope Clayton or Brad finds another concealed door in the plaster."

As he was speaking, Mercedes felt metal on the wood. "No way," she muttered. She ran her fingers over it again. "Quincy, you won't believe this. See if you think it's part of the bookcase construction or a latch."

He grinned at her wide eyes and came to investigate. With a push on the metal, the bookcase shifted inwards. Mercedes helped him shove it after it stuck, and they found themselves in a long, narrow, dark space. Dust rose from the floorboards, disturbed by the bookcase door.

Tammy walked into the bedroom to ask Mercedes and Quincy what they wanted for lunch, which she was preparing in the kitchen. She saw the opening in the bookcases and came to see where they were. After her eyes adjusted to the shadows, she screamed.

The first thing Mercedes noticed when they forced the old bookcase open was an odor. Then she saw bulky shapes, some covered, like home décor items stored in a closet. Heavy dust swirled under their shoes and made her sneeze. But beside her, Quincy froze. She turned to see what stopped him and clapped her hand to her mouth in horror.

Time seemed to stand still as she took in details of the scene before her, and her heart raced. She felt a rush of lightheadedness, then thought her knees might buckle, so she reached to put her hand on the wall. This kept her steady as her eyes roamed over the dreadful messages written in blood all over the walls at one end of the narrow, shadowy space, a record left to tell the tale of a crime of passion, a confession of brutal revenge, and a vile voodoo curse over the long-departed soul of a man whose bones remained hidden here.

As if in a dream, she heard Tammy's scream. But she was rooted in the shadows when Tammy ran away, her screams reverberating in the empty house. Mercedes could not move, immersed in the hideous scene and the evidence that remained of an evil pagan ritual.

Brad's boots echoed in her ears when he ran to the bookcase on the creaking plank floor. Then she heard his voice behind her, over her shoulder. He called on heaven under his breath, but for help, not as a curse word.

Quincy was the calmest one of the three. He had shaken off his shock and started squatting down slowly, using his cellphone camera to capture the scene. He reached behind to touch Mercedes, and she bent to clasp his hand. "Mercedes," he said in a soothing, steady tone. "Please go call the police. Tell them it's not an emergency, but we have stumbled on evidence of a Civil War era murder and need an investigation team out here."

She gulped, and he turned slightly in the narrow space to see if she was okay. Nodding, she stammered. "Yes—yes. I can do that." Taking a step back, she bumped into Brad. She gasped and jumped, but he steadied her with his hands on her shoulders and helped her take a few steps to the bookcase opening, where she gulped deep breaths of air in the very ordinary, boring old room.

Her handprint showed on the dirty window, an encouraging reminder of her connection to Tonya's old Granny. Granny was praying for her, she was sure of it. Mercedes took one unsteady step toward the only door in the room, toward Tammy's hysterical sobs and Clayton's soothing, unintelligible words.

When she made it to the doorframe, she paused and held on to it, tears stinging her eyes and sobs rising in her throat. But she pushed the scene from her mind and focused on what Quincy asked. He was protecting her, trying to get her away from the horror and give her a means of helping. She would call the police. Then she needed to go to Tammy, whose cries were fainter now as Clayton took her down the stairs.

Dazed, she went to the first front bedroom she came to and looked out the watery panes of the window to the street below. It was so normal, and the view grounded her again. Reality was what she saw outside, an ordinary day in the summer sunshine for the neighbors who were walking their dogs and jogging. With another deep breath to steady herself, she reached for her phone and dropped it. The smack and echo it made in the emptiness on the wood floor jolted her, and she choked back another sob.

When she picked the phone up again, it took several unsteady attempts before she touched the right numbers on the screen to reach the police. In a tight voice that sounded strange in her own ears, she repeated what Quincy told her to say and gave them Tammy and Clayton's address.

Then she ended the call and cried. That is where Quincy found her.

Brad directed his demolition crew to another job site and Quincy brought Mercedes down to stay with Tammy. When Mercedes ran to the bathroom to vomit, Tammy shook off her own distress and became angry. "It's no wonder she's sick, after seeing that devil stuff!" She waved her apron to send Quincy off. "You go on up with Brad and Clayton. Tell the police what happened, I'll take care of the poor girl."

Clucking like a mother hen, she got a damp towel to take to Mercedes. Reluctant to leave, Quincy backed to the staircase. "I'll be down as soon as I can. Try giving her peppermint tea or ginger tea, or ginger ale if you have any. She's not allergic to that."

Tammy knocked on the bathroom door and Mercedes told her to come in. She stood at the sink, rinsing out her mouth and washing her face. Her host offered her a slightly damp towel with the faint scent of peppermint oil on it, and Mercedes gratefully held it to her face while Tammy searched a cabinet and brought out a package with a new toothbrush in it.

"You might want this, and I've got the kettle boiling for some peppermint tea," she said, patting Mercedes' arm. "I don't have ginger ale stocked yet. When you feel better, come on in the kitchen and sit with me."

When Mercedes came out, the suntan was back in her complexion, and she was somber but calm. She sat in front of a cup of tea while Tammy put lunch back in the refrigerator. "No one will feel like eating until the police leave," she said in a practical tone.

They both started when the warbling front doorbell rang. "What now?" Tammy muttered, and she patted Mercedes on the shoulder as she passed to answer the door. She came back in with her young neighbor Tonya and the gray-haired older woman Mercedes had met through the upstairs window.

Tammy introduced her as Tonya's Granny. Tonya said, "We knew you locked the back gate, so we walked down the block and came in the front."

Tammy asked them to sit down and to pardon the awkward circumstances at the house. She said that if anyone would understand what they were going through, it should be Tonya and Granny, and she was glad they had come. Ever the hostess, she offered them something to eat, and Tonya's eyes lit up at a small plate of fresh-baked cookies on the table.

"When we saw the police were here again, we expected you found old Jack," Granny said, accepting a cup of tea, her sharp eyes studying Tammy and Mercedes. "Don't you get upset, now. It was better to know than to live here and not know, like the others did."

Tammy pressed a hand to her mouth and looked away. Granny reached out to pat her arm. "There's nothin' to fear from him now, dear. He's long gone to his judgement, and he can't come back. I've prayed for this day most of my life, for Christians to come live here with the light of Jesus to drive away the darkness. You're the answer to my prayers and I hope you'll stay."

Tammy blinked back tears and took Granny's hand. "Thank you for telling me. Yes, it's best to know. It never occurred to me that anyone was praying for us to buy this house, or that Jesus blended our prayers to accomplish the same answer. And here I've been thinking we should get away from it. I don't know if I've ever been the answer to anyone's prayers before, except of course my husband."

With a weak smile, she turned to Mercedes. "Granny, I'm afraid Mercedes and I have had a nasty shock. We're shaken, and she got sick. It was horrible, just horrible. Not something I can talk about."

Granny watched Mercedes sip the peppermint tea. "Yes, the woman with the glowing halo of hair and eyes like a meadow. Tonya told you my story, handed down to my family for many years. We waited for you, and those who would come and reveal this today. You saw something evil, something that grieves the Holy Spirit who dwells in you. But it was not the first time, and it won't be the last, for that is your destiny. We are all called in different ways."

Quincy and Clayton peeked into the kitchen, then opened the door wide. "Everything okay here?" Clayton asked, and Quincy came to stand by Mercedes. He put his hand on her shoulder. "Feeling better?"

Mercedes nodded and smiled weakly, touching his hand with hers where it rested on her shoulder. Tammy introduced Tonya and Granny, explaining that they were back yard neighbors.

Clayton looked at Granny. "You're the one who has the story of what happened here, right? As far as we can tell, it looks like the gardener's tale is true and he sealed his revenge with a curse on the victim, but not the property. I don't want to frighten Tonya with the details, but when we have a report, I'll let you know what the news coverage doesn't tell. You can decide if it's the same as your family story."

Granny nodded. "When they get everything out of the hidden hallway and open it again, all will be well. I hope you'll stay and make this a place of hospitality and peace, and that you'll allow me to bring my pastor and Christian friends over to pray blessings over it."

She rose and walked over to Mercedes and Quincy, putting her hands on their shoulders, and bowing her head to pray. "Oh Lord, may your hand of grace, mercy, blessing and anointing rest on these warriors in Your service, bound with you in a cord no evil can break. Grant them Your peace in every path You lead them on. Amen."

Then Granny went to Clayton and Tammy, taking their hands. "Oh Lord, may your grace, mercy, blessing and anointing rest on this couple as they seek to share your light in this place. Grant them peace. Amen."

Hearing the door open quietly behind them, everyone turned to see Brad in the doorway with a police officer. The officer grinned instantly at the sight of Granny, and she held out her arms to him. He quickly stepped in to hug her. "Granny, I should've known you'd be here! I hoped I'd get to be one up on you and break the news."

She patted him on the back and let go, looking up at him sharply. "Are you okay?"

He wiped a sheen of sweat from his forehead. "It was rough, Granny. I ain't gonna lie. But he wrote the confession in blood, and his story, so we know what happened. It's finally over."

The officer turned to the others, putting his arm around Granny. "Granny here is a close relative, but not really my grandma. I'm among the pack of wild kids who spent a lot of time in her house, and I owe her too much to repay. We go to church together."

He looked at Mercedes with kind eyes. "Miss Ellison, Mr. Holmwood told me you're not feeling well after the shock. If you want to make a statement later, he has my card. When I saw you here the morning that we investigated the break in, I hoped it meant all this would come to light. But I'm truly sorry you had to experience it."

Mercedes nodded her thanks and drew a deep breath. "It was the voodoo curse ceremony, and the messages written on the wall that got me. Vengeance was all the justice Sirena's brother thought his sister would ever get."

Chapter 10

You are the light of the world. A city situated on a hill cannot be hidden.
Matthew 5:14

"Something happened again today that confirmed what I read in my Great-Great Grand Aunt's journal," said Mercedes as she sat with Quincy, Lois, and Aaron by the pool. She turned to Quincy and gripped his hand as he held hers on the patio table. "Granny said something odd about waiting on me to come for this day, this revelation of what happened, and that such things are my destiny. She doesn't know me and Quincy, yet her prayer was as if she had read the journal entry about the time my aunt spent with her grandmother the same night a man murdered her. Her grandmother raised her to consider how a cord of three, made of a couple committed to following Jesus, was unbreakable."

"That's amazing, Mercedes. What did she pray for?" asked Lois.

Quincy said, "That the Lord's hand of grace, mercy, blessing and anointing rest on us as warriors in His service, that He would give us peace as we walk with Him and bind us in a cord that no evil can break."

Aaron nodded and glanced at Lois with a knowing look passing between them. "Granny is insightful about heavenly things. A few rare individuals live among us like ordinary people, yet their minds are on things so much higher than the passing winds of worldly things."

"What else have you read from the journal?" asked Lois.

"I only came into possession of it recently, and so much is happening that I can't dedicate the time it deserves to read it. I limited myself to scanning a few pages for random things she wrote, like quotes and scripture she was focusing on. My grandfather wants to know what she had to say about the night things went so wrong there—or so right, depending on your perspective, I suppose. But I passed by those pages. I want to save them for when I'm visiting back home soon, or for when I return after the summer is over. I can read those entries with him and get his wisdom and insight, his perspective on how this all fits with our family history."

The foursome sat pondering this quietly for several minutes while the day changed into evening, like a missionary taking light into the darkness on the other side of the world. A frog sang a croaking song to his mate in the bubbling rock fountain and insects intermittently began the hum, buzz, crackle, rattle, and chirp of their evening symphony around the elephant ears, banana trees, citrus trees, and palms in the garden. And suddenly, the brass gleamed on lanterns that came on all at once, and the pool glowed turquoise blue as the timer triggered the underwater lights.

The lights coming on in the darkness sparked Mercedes' raw emotions and her eyes stung with unshed tears. It had been a hard day, with so much to unpack about the Popplewell house. She found Quincy watching her. Then he looked over the patio table at the older couple.

"I don't know if Mercedes has ever mentioned any of her recommendations about renovating the interior of the house in Savannah. But I've seen them. All along, before she went into the house for the first time, she based some ideas for a place of hospitality on interviews with the clients. Tammy mentioned wanting to be a light, as the Bible describes what God's people are on earth. I heard Tammy say the same thing one day as she wondered if she had misunderstood the Lord's direction for them to buy the property. She didn't see how her calling to be light could overcome the darkness being uncovered on that property, and she was ready to put it on the market again. But if she looks back at the floor plan Mercedes suggested, she will find the entire hidden hallway was to be restored, anyway."

"Really?" asked Aaron, leaning forward on his elbows, his eyes sparking with the interest of a contractor with a renovation ahead. "What are your plans?"

Mercedes took a sip of lemonade and cleared her throat. "I wanted to take the house back to what I believe the original architect designed the heart of it to be. They lost his records in the chaos in Savannah during the war, but it's clear to me that his focus was on a grand entryway and staircase. It was a welcoming place made to embrace guests. The unscrupulous carpetbagger reconfigured several things that corrupted and scarred the house's heart—he closed off and concealed doors to storage in the basement and under the stair landing, damaged the landing floor to create a secret storage area to sell from, and it was criminal the way he closed the upper hallway to make that awful room with the bookcase access. There's a geometric cutout on the first floor from the landing to the next floor, where he had the beautiful, open hallway to the staircase and first floor closed in. So, my suggestions for Tammy and Clayton are to open and restore that open hallway again and add skylights through the attic to make the area airy."

She met Quincy's eyes. "I don't think they can or should restore that stairway. It makes no sense financially and now, knowing what we found, it needs to come out of the house altogether."

Then she turned back to Lois and Aaron. "I went a different direction than the original architect and suggested they replace it with one that uses the beautiful flourishes of iron scrollwork on the front of the house on the railings of a new staircase. I would also open a second-floor bedroom across from the stairway and make it an elegant but cozy sitting room, full of light from French doors, with space for a reading corner and a small antique desk for guests who need to work while on vacation."

"Oh!" gasped Aaron. "Lois showed me a photo of the front of that house on the internet. Are you saying that opening the upstairs hallway and using your idea of ironwork railings will create the look of a balcony, of sorts, like the second-floor front exterior of the house?"

"Exactly, keeping the Spanish-Caribbean personality and theme running throughout. The sitting room I mentioned at the top of the stairs would open to the second-story porch balcony on the front, so it would be functional again. I realize the look is more like New Orleans, but there is a lot of black ironwork exterior décor around Savannah, too."

"I believe doing all this would make Tammy and Clayton move on," announced Lois. "They won't even recall what it was like when they bought it."

Quincy sighed. "First, the Popplewells must decide what to do next. Putting the property on the market again isn't off the table, and Tammy relented today because Mercedes was sick. A care-giver switch went off inside her and her screams changed to anger at what caused Mercedes to be so upset. That, and Granny's visit, was the only reason they didn't decide to sell today."

Mercedes and Quincy sat on the half-moon steps on the shallow end of Lois' pool, relaxing after swimming laps, enjoying the night sky and the enchanting setting of romantic lighting around the water. The takeout meal and conversation with Lois and Aaron when they came back from Savannah soothed her spirits, and she thought sleep would come after all.

Beside her, Quincy leaned in to bump her shoulder gently. "A few days ago, you wanted to help bring the mystery of the Popplewell house to light. You said you had scenarios playing in your head. Did it turn out as you expected?"

Sighing, Mercedes idly stirred the water with her foot. "Yes, but I tried to be fair to Haute, allowing for Sirena's brother to have killed her, catching her sneaking out and accidentally ending her life trying to stop her. He still had reason for revenge on the carpetbagger on her behalf. All I had was Granny's story, through Tonya, from the brother's perspective. Would he confess if he killed his sister accidentally and buried her under the floor? That was an unknown."

She slid further down into the water, reaching to push a fallen oak leaf around with her toe. "But in that awful hidden hallway, Sirena's brother left his testimony about what happened, why he killed Haute and performed a ceremony to curse him. He literally wrote it on the walls, partly in the man's blood. When Sirena was shouting at Haute after finding him in their bed with another woman, she claimed she was newly pregnant and it was time to make her mistress of the house, as he promised. Her brother heard the shouting and ran out into the yard, then overheard the murder before Haute threatened him with a gun and ran him off the property. The other woman was a witness to what he couldn't see when she screamed and said Sirena was dead, and she had to get home to her husband before someone discovered her at a crime scene."

"Sirena's brother knew he couldn't help her if she was dead, so he left to get authorities," said Quincy. "He wrote on the walls that no one would go to the house, no one would help him. So, he took matters into his own hands and then left to join the former homeowners in New Orleans, assuming he ever found them. That's a long way to go in a war-ravaged country. All we know for sure is he left Savannah, because Granny's people never saw him after that."

"Isn't it interesting that he didn't know about the hidden hallway? I suppose he never went inside anymore and only knew Jack hired a carpenter to do remodeling. He wrote in his confession that he sneaked into the house at night and found the carpetbagger in the middle of stuffing stolen goods into the room, with the bookcase door open and some lanterns burning. That's when he killed him, then did the ceremony in the room and sealed him up in it like a tomb. No one could prove he killed Jack Haute, until, as he wrote, 'the house comes down in the future.'"

"I believe him," Quincy said. "The art and other things in that room may not prove to be in good condition after so long, but it had a price in those days. He left gold coins in an open strongbox, along with the account ledger and other things. Sirena's brother wanted nothing but revenge."

"Right. Good point. I have a lot of speculation, assumptions, and guesses, but it will be good to see the coroner's reports and other analysis of the evidence."

Quincy reached for her arm and pulled her closer. "It didn't surprise you at finding evidence of the murder. I could tell that when you talked to Brad about the hallway. What upset you were the occult aspects. I admit, it was over the top, a sure sign of passion on Sirena's brother's part. I've seen a lot of things in dig sites, but this unnerved me, too. And all the bloody writing, the confession and testimony on the walls, the words of the curse and all the occult objects—I wish you didn't have that memory."

"It was horrifying, but I needed to know because Tammy saw it, too. Maybe I needed to know because of something the Lord wants me to understand and face in the future."

He stroked her arm soothingly in the silky water. "Will you be able to sleep tonight? I'm sure Lois will let you use her guest room if you need to."

Mercedes smiled and pulled herself to sit up beside him. She leaned into his shoulder. "If you can sleep after dealing with a day like this, I can, too. Just leave your phone on and close by on your bed in case I need to call for reassurance."

On the small table beside a pool lounge chair, Mercedes' phone vibrated and notified her of a message. She lifted her sunglasses and adjusted to the phone in her hand to eliminate the glare on the screen. "It's from Tammy," she announced.

In the next lounge chair, Quincy looked up from his laptop. "Oh, yeah? Are we being fired or summoned?"

Mercedes studied the screen. "Well... it's a long message for a text. She could have called and been faster. Hang on."

He waited while she read everything. She looked up and smiled. "Can you finish up online and go to Savannah with me by noon? I have a date with Brad."

Quincy snorted. "Not a chance you're going to meet hunky Brad without me. Does this mean you still have a job?"

Airily, she waved a hand. "Brad wants to discuss specifics on my plans for gutting the hallway and staircase and opening that sitting room to the balcony. Law enforcement and the historical society cleaned everything out this morning. Tammy doesn't want a trace of the crimes or the carpetbagger's goods left on the premises."

Quincy set his laptop on the table, applauded Mercedes, and stood with his hand out to take hers. "I'm so proud of you and what a stunning place the Popplewell house will become. When you're busy with the construction schedule, remember to save time for all the summer fun we planned to have while we're here."

"I won't forget what you gave up and how far you traveled to be with me, and time with you is at the top of my priority list," she said as he pulled her into his arms. "I can't imagine doing this project without you."

He kissed her temple and murmured, "I'm thankful that you don't have to."

To Readers

Did you like this novel? You can enjoy previews of the rest of this inspirational suspense series at the end of this book and continue the adventures of Mercedes Ellison. Remember to help other readers by sharing your review!

To sample the next novella in the Strange Sands Suspense series, **The Freedom Staircase**, look for the free excerpt to get you started at the end of this book.

If you'd like to know more about the inspiration and research for this series, check the **Resources** on the next page. Leaders of book clubs may find the **Discussion Topics** page helpful.

Stay updated with me via my fun-packed author newsletter and websites at Southern Sky Publishing[1] and Pamela Poole Fine Art[2], or join me on YouTube[3], Goodreads[4] and BookBub[5].

---

1. http://www.southernskypublishing.com
2. http://www.pamelapoole.com
3. https://www.youtube.com/channel/UC9aV3zHRlASXUUBEF7xbT9Q
4. https://www.goodreads.com/author/show/3934732.Pamela_Poole
5. https://www.bookbub.com/profile/pamela-poole

Resources

Biblical and Historical Perspectives on the Supernatural
There are so many! Here are the ones where I find the most helpful research material for both reliable, quick references and for in-depth Bible Study and Biblical Worldview writing. I'm sure readers have favorites they would add to this list, but there may be a new one for you on this list.

YouTube has many podcast interviews and conference presentations with Dr. Michael S. Heiser about the Bible, but those who want to dig deeper will discover a lot of extra material and primary sources on this scholar's main website. I highly recommend his videos on the Divine Council and Cosmic Geography:
Dr. Michael S. Heiser[6]

Christian Women's Podcast for Apologetics and Worldview
Melissa Dougherty (author of Happy Lies)

---

6. https://drmsh.com/

Architecture

The main character in the Strange Sands Inspirational Suspense Series is an Architectural Historian. Her workplace sets the stage for most of the stories. In the second novella, The Hidden Hallway, Savannah Georgia is the setting. The Popplewell house does not fit the descriptions in the most popular architectural styles in the city, but those are mentioned, and readers can find them in the first link. The Popplewell house is a real house in Savannah that I've photographed and painted in my studio. The painting is in the book and on my artist websites.

Savannah's Architectural Styles[7]

In the third novella in the series, the main setting is a Lowcountry Plantation in Charleston County, north of Charleston toward Francis Marion National Forest. My descriptions for the mansion and grounds of Majestic Oaks are inspired loosely by a real plantation that readers can visit. I also recommend books by Archibald Rutledge, South Carolina's first Poet Laurate and descendant of the original plantation owners in the early 1700's. I have two, Home by the River and Life's Extras. His descriptions of life at the plantation are informative and poignant. He donated Hampton Plantation and it is now a historic park. Included in the novella is my painting of the Washington Oak from a photo I took there when I visited in 2010.

---

7. https://www.savannah.com/savannahs-architectural-styles/

<u>Hampton Plantation</u>[8]
Home by the River by Archibald Rutledge
(the book that earned him a Nobel Prize Nomination)

---

8. https://south-carolina-plantations.com/charleston/hampton.html

Discussion Topics

If you read the first novella in this series, The Old Cedar Chest, what was your impression of the Prologue event? In the third novella in the series, *The Freedom Staircase,* Mercedes Ellison's grandparents tell her more about that night, and she reads aloud to them the journal entry her Great-Great Grand Aunt Mercedes wrote. How does your faith background, or lack of one, contribute to what you think about the encounter between Claire Ellison and Roland Lenoir in the year 1900?

How would you like to see the cycle of vengeance on the part of the Lenoir family end?

Readers may be familiar with growing up in broken relationships and dysfunction, as in the Lenoir family. Some cycles go on for several generations before a family member decides to follow Christ and break out of the cycle. I heard a testimony yesterday in church by a pastor who did this. Do you have a story like this that you can share?

There are many inspiring accounts of events and poignant family challenges of survival during all of America's wartime years. People act on the faith and beliefs they have, right or wrong, true or false, good or bad. In *The Hidden Hallway*, we see how a change in the choices of several characters might give the story a different outcome. Discuss where you think the story might have gone a different direction.

Were there any parts of the story that you plan to explore further? Examples are: New Age influences in today's church, occult activity among today's Christians, and what happens to a Christian believer when he or she passes from this world into eternity.

How many Bible references in this story did you look up? I recommend using a Study Bible and online commentaries to make sure you are grounding the verses in their context to glean the full meaning. It is common for people to take a verse and build a wrong belief on it.

I interviewed Christian believers about some of their supernatural experiences and have listened to many such stories from the mission field. We should never "educate" ourselves out of believing the realities of the spiritual realm around us and the miracles we see every day. Have you had, or heard of, an experience where an encounter or outcome could only be explained as divine intervention?

About the Author

Pamela Poole writes inspirational mystery and suspense that explore the intersection of faith, history, and the unseen spiritual realm. Her stories are grounded in a clear Christian worldview and shaped by a deep respect for both history and biblical truth.

Pamela writes inspirational stories that bring together Christian faith, historic places, and hidden truths. Her novels reveal how the past can press into the present, where faith becomes essential to discernment and courage. Her characters are ordinary people facing extraordinary challenges, learning to trust Jesus when darkness threatens and answers are not easily found.

The Strange Sands Suspense series and the Painter Place Saga blend richly detailed settings with themes of calling, obedience, redemption, and spiritual warfare. Pamela's fiction offers clean, thought-provoking suspense designed both to engage the imagination and to encourage the heart. When she isn't writing, Pamela enjoys research, painting in her art studio and on location along the Southern coast and making memories with her family and friends.

The Strange Sands Novella Series

The Old Cedar Chest, Strange Sands Suspense 1
Hilton Head

An antique cedar hope chest.
A hidden document.
A century-spanning vendetta.

The Old Cedar Chest launches a faith-filled suspense novella series following architectural historian Mercedes Annalee Ellison as she uncovers the unexplainable forces tied to historic properties—and her own family legacy.

Mercedes never expected her great-great-grandaunt's fragile journal and a tattered manila envelope to change her life. Yet the miraculous way they came into her possession—and the unease they stir in her spirit—would give even the most hardened skeptic pause.

Before she can meet her first client or settle into what she hopes will be a quiet summer at a Lowcountry cottage, an ominous shadow stretches across her carefully planned future. Mercedes soon realizes she is the target of a vendetta that goes back more than a century. Time is running out, and survival may mean accepting a calling she never sought and a destiny bound to the legendary Ellison family.

In this heart-pounding Christian suspense novella, Mercedes must rely on more than her education and instincts. Anchored in faith and surrounded by eerie revelations, she learns God equips ordinary people to stand firm against extraordinary challenges. Filled with mystery, history, and spiritual depth, The Old Cedar Chest invites readers to consider how faith, courage, and divine purpose intersect in life's unseen battles.

The Hidden Hallway, Strange Sands Suspense 2
Savannah

An antebellum house.
A hidden hallway.
A tale of passion and revenge.

In *The Hidden Hallway*, architectural historian Mercedes Annalee Ellison faces another assignment that challenges not only her professional expertise but her spiritual resolve. Tammy and Clayton Popplewell hired Mercedes as they registered and renovated an antebellum house in the beautiful Southern city of Savannah, Georgia. But she knows this is not the boring job she hoped for when she arrives on the first day to find the local police there. What should have been a routine assessment of aging blueprints and structural quirks takes a chilling turn when Mercedes uncovers a concealed hallway that doesn't appear on any original plans.

As Mercedes investigates the history of the property, she must rely not only on her expertise but on God's guidance to discern something hidden—and why it matters now. When neighbors seek her out with a strange Civil War Era tale of passion and revenge, she works to uncover a terrifying darkness and help her clients make the house into the inn where they dream of sharing light—before they give up and she loses the job.

The Hidden Hallway is a gripping Christian inspirational suspense novella blending history, mystery, and spiritual warfare. Set against the rich atmosphere of historic Savannah, it's a story of faith tested, dreams endangered, and the assurance that God is always present—especially where secrets hide.

The Freedom Staircase, Strange Sands Suspense 3
Charleston

An Enduring Lowcountry Plantation.
A Legendary Patriot Refuge.
A Last Stand for Freedom.

It thrilled Mercedes Ellison to be chosen to work as an architectural historian for Majestic Oaks, a plantation that endured and survived wars on American soil. The stately Georgian mansion features the Freedom Staircase, where legendary patriots stopped for refuge in their roles with the Continental Army in the American Revolution. Her client needs help to keep the plantation he inherited, which is steeped in the history of the Lowcountry of South Carolina, home of the Swamp Fox and four signers of the Declaration of Independence.

There are also some unsolved mysteries on the property. Bringing them to light will help her client, and she finds clues in a secret passage used by the patriots. But then her archenemy dies in jail, and his son watches her. The long-standing vendetta against the Ellison family that began in *The Old Cedar Chest* now escalates, and Mercedes knows the danger she faces is real, personal, and relentless. Can she make a last stand for freedom from the past that began with the murder of her ancestor on a stormy night in England?

Blending historical intrigue, Christian faith, and suspense, *The Freedom Staircase* is an inspirational story of legacy, obedience, and the courage to walk the path God sets before us, even when it leads straight through danger.

The Dark Passage, Strange Sands Suspense 4
Bluffton

Faith tested.
Purpose questioned.
Evil revealed.

Mercedes Ellison is hoping for a quiet summer as she plans her wedding—boring clients, simple renovations, no surprises. But the Marlowe House is anything but ordinary.

Doran Marlowe, a former missionary guide, has spent decades traveling the world's most remote regions. His shuttered passageway and unsettling artwork hint at experiences he never fully left behind. His sister, Mary Lou, newly returned from the mission field, carries her own burdens—discouragement, doubt, and unanswered questions about her calling.

When a terrifying incident shatters the calm of the historic home, Mercedes finds herself drawn into a mystery that defies logic and explanation. The danger feels personal, spiritual, and disturbingly familiar.

In *The Dark Passage*, Pamela Poole weaves a faith-filled suspense story that confronts spiritual darkness with biblical truth. This inspirational mystery asks hard questions about obedience, spiritual authority, and trusting God when the unseen world breaks into the ordinary.

The Devil's Drawer, Strange Sands Suspense 5
Beaufort

An ominous oath taken for personal privilege.
An enigmatic artifact unbound by time and place.
An evil consequence for generations.

A chilling mystery unfolds at Seashell Cottage as architectural historian Mercedes Ellison stumbles upon an ominous black cabinet decorated with ancient Egyptian symbols. Delivered under the cover of darkness, this enigmatic artifact pulls her and her client into a web of secrets that stretches across generations.

As they delve deeper, a private investigator friend joins them in unraveling the sinister connection between the cabinet and a long-buried family oath to a clandestine society. With blood as the ultimate spiritual currency, they must confront the haunting legacy of a deceased ancestor whose evil choices ripple through time, binding Mercedes' client in ways they never imagined.

This gripping story is filled with mystery and revelations. As a Christian, Mercedes knows Jesus reverses curses. But will her client come to know this before it is too late?

In *The Devil's Drawer,* Pamela Poole weaves a faith-filled suspense story that confronts spiritual darkness with biblical truth. This inspirational mystery asks hard questions about spiritual authority and trusting God when the unseen world breaks into the ordinary.

Grab your copy today and join Mercedes on this thrilling adventure!

Coming in 2026!

The Black Hourglass, Strange Sands Suspense 6
St. Augustine

In the shadow lies the truth.

A hidden letter.
A stolen fortune.
A secret that refused to stay buried.

Quincy Holmwood thought his work in St. Augustine was over until a cryptic message from a church archivist pulled him back into a mystery from 1688. How can he resist a search for the truth left by a murdered friar about hidden evidence of a crime against the Crown, committed by a powerful group of colonial settlers of America's oldest city? The trail of clues had endured for the courageous man of a future generation who was bold enough to follow them. With his fiancée, **Mercedes Ellison**, and a small archaeology team, Quincy races to decode symbols and clues tied to a forgotten brotherhood whose emblem—the **black hourglass**—marks the flow of time the brotherhood believed was under their control.
The brotherhood's final heir is watching his progress.

And he never wants the past to come to light.
As accidents turn deadly, Quincy must rely on his faith and the conviction that he is the one the friar believed would someday reveal the truth.
What was hidden in darkness was never meant to stay there.

Here's your FREE peek of Book 3 in the series!

The Freedom Staircase

Strange Sands Suspense 2
Excerpt from Chapter 1

The Spirit-filled life is not a special, deluxe edition of Christianity. It is part and parcel of the total plan of God for His people.
-A. W. Tozer

Mercedes was excited about working with clients to evaluate a plantation mansion with a feature called the Freedom Staircase, and she was in no mood to debate the Patriot cause in the American Revolution with a guy who was half British. In her opinion, her boyfriend had a serious gap in his history education and needed to take another look now that he lived in the Lowcountry of South Carolina, home of the Swamp Fox and four signers of the Declaration of Independence.

She rubbed the tension over her brows. "I don't want to argue, Quincy. Frankly, I doubt you could understand this. You may have been born here in America, but you spent your life mainly with the British side of your family and traveling the world to archaeology sites. Strong opinions about patriotism come from the heart more than the head. Let's just agree to disagree."

Quincy jerked back his head to cushions on the pale gray leather sofa and looked heavenward, as if praying for patience.

"If this issue is so dear to your heart, Mercedes, I want to understand it in my head. The people called 'rebels' as patriots in the Revolution were divided less than one hundred years later, insulting citizens as being 'rebels' who supported Southern independence and state sovereignty. Families and friends became mortal enemies."

Mercedes huffed. "Now you're going into another era, and wow, that's an interesting accusation, since Great Britain's history is packed with wars in which families and friends became treacherous enemies and royalty killed family members to keep power and a throne. Maybe the colonists got used to that from living in England?"

She rose from her seat beside him. "My patriotic interest in this job is the American Revolution, the Patriots, Sons of Liberty, Whigs, and, yes, rebels. They wanted the Loyalists, Royalists, Tories, and King's Friends—anyone loyal to the British—to remain here as a valuable part of society. Like the Civil War, less than one hundred years later, yes, families got torn apart. I'm going back to work now."

He quickly reached for her hand. "I'm sorry our lunch break turned into this debate, and it's my fault. Please, sit back down."

With a sigh, Mercedes perched on the edge of the sofa. He gently tugged her arm, pulling her closer to him. "I'll look into this and fill in that gap in my education, okay? You're right, I spent little time in American history other than events and dates, and I focused on ancient things, studying whatever I needed wherever I was in the world. It's high time I learned about my country."

She nodded. He tried to keep the pleading tone out of his voice. "I don't need a desk and extra screen this afternoon. Let's take our laptops out to the Carolina room and work by the river view."

Mercedes was moody, withdrawn, and distracted. Quincy watched her out of the corner of his eye as she sat nearby in an ample white wicker chair with her bare feet on the wide, matching stool. She rested against fabric cushions printed with palm fronds in tropical shades of blue. If he was a painter, he would ask her to pose like this.

But her mind was back in the 1700s, he could tell. Ever since she started working on the plantation mansion job yesterday, she was somewhere else—and he was jealous. He did not understand her distraction. In his frustration, he had picked a fight with her. It was stupid on his part. He knew better than to demean the importance of America's founding and the role of heroes from the Lowcountry. She would drop a guy for less than that. The words were out of his mouth before he used his brain, and it would be no easy feat to regain her esteem.

He followed her up to Charleston for this job, unwilling to stay in his carriage house summer rental without her being two doors down in a cottage. She was planning to stay here with her family for a week and drive up to the plantation when needed. His family had not settled in their Charleston property, and he accepted the invitation to stay in the Ellison's guest cottage while she was home. It was a chance to engage his ulterior motive to spend time with her brother and parents again, talking to them about his plans for the future, and a welcome way to be with her without the restrictions of living in separate places in Bluffton.

The idyllic plans he had of getting closer to her were now mere castles in the air. He was not important enough to sidetrack her from wherever she went in her mind and heart with that plantation. If he wanted to be on her radar, he needed to do some research or be an attentive student when she shared her work.

He opted for the tactic of being a student. "Since Majestic Oaks is rich in history, why are the owners not trying to make it a state park or museum?"

Mercedes looked up from her laptop screen, and he waited as her eyes cleared from wherever she had been in her mind. She stretched one pretty foot on the wicker stool, pointing and flexing her blue pedicured toes. "They need to sell before the long process of fundraising and clearing red tape, but they hope to find a buyer who will keep it working instead of selling off the land. So far, the state is only interested in the house and immediate grounds. The family wants as much of the property as possible to remain with the house. They have sold chunks of it over the years, so it's a fraction of what it was when it was built as a rice plantation."

"Someone's been living there?"

She shifted her laptop computer and glanced over at him. "Yes, most of the time. It was being rented out by the last owner, a great-uncle who was in declining health and had to go live with one of my clients the past year. The tenants were friends of the family, staying on as a favor for the owner, though they did well, cultivating the landscaping nurseries and other agriculture on the property and maintaining the old mansion. They could lease those portions out to entrepreneurs who don't have deep pockets. The property is by a river, so there are resources to manage. But the current renters are aging and ready to retire, so it works out for all concerned to sell."

Quincy raised a dark brow. "Have there been any historical dig sites on the grounds?"

Mercedes grinned at his archaeological curiosity. "Not enough, and if you're interested, we could ask about investigating. They have occasional educational tours and some college groups out, but they all seem focused on the environment, not on preserving history. Some metal detector clubs have gotten permission to search a few areas around the old slave quarters. Not all plantations were cruel places and many of the slaves at Majestic Oaks stayed there after emancipation in the Civil War. The master of the house went off to the battlefields, and the loyal, long-time slaves tried to protect the big house from possible plundering by Union soldiers. They took furnishings in boats down the river, and they returned many after the war. I'll see those when I go out there tomorrow. But according to family records, in the confusion, the family silver and some other valuables never were found. Ever since, owners tried digging up the most likely spots to search for these heirlooms, but maybe they failed because these were the likely locations. There is no written record of all the generals and troops who came through, though some were in the area."

He shifted in his chair. "Was anything found by the metal detector club?"

"Oh, yes. Coins, interesting buttons, and so on. A few of the families stayed on for generations, and the owners called them guardian angels of the plantation and best friends they grew up with. Some were so well respected by both the owners and workers that they became valuable foremen."

"If you can get permission, I'd like to go out with some equipment and a map of the property. Any cemeteries?"

She nodded. "You bet. They dedicated one to the slaves and workers who lived there, so the people who didn't choose burial at their church cemeteries had a place on the plantation. They liked to be laid to rest by water, so this one is above what used to be the spring flood boundaries. Of course, that's a consideration in the property's sale and the cemetery has its own road for families to access it. The family has maintained it over the years, so the surrounding forest hasn't taken over."

"If I clear my schedule, do you mind if I ride up with you to the Oaks? Unless having a tag-along will make you look unprofessional."

Mercedes studied him suspiciously. "Of course, you can come along. I'm only meeting with one client, and he inherited the largest portion of the estate. His two cousins aren't in town. Wallace is laid-back and genuine to talk to. Why are you suddenly interested in the plantation?"

He shrugged. "I've always learned history better hands-on."

Wallace Hampton snorted and kicked a pinecone the size of his fist out of the driveway. "The way the government spends my tax money is an immoral disaster. They won't do any better managing my family plantation. If it weren't for my cousins,

I'd make this work instead of selling out, but I understand their reasons. One says her special-needs grandbaby needs a surgery that insurance won't cover, and the other cousin says he has become disabled. Both need the money for out-of-control medical bills. They've never lived here, never even visited, and I never met them. Their families married off a couple generations ago and didn't return. I appreciate Mary takin' my uncle in the last year, though. That's why she got a portion."

He shook his head and heaved a deep sigh. "It ain't no secret I got the mansion and the biggest share in the plantation by far, and I'd move back up here in a minute and take over. But I can't pay them off their part. I'm stuck between a rock and a hard place, and this truly breaks my heart."

Mercedes said, "I gathered this from our emails. Thanks for agreeing to meet me here without the real estate agent, so you can share your feelings about it and fill me in on all the things I'd miss behind the scenes. You said the agent is urging you to consider some aggressive buyers who are offering much less than the value. Does she think your appraiser is wrong, or is she expecting the property will be on the market for a long time?"

Hampton shook his head again and scowled. "I'll be honest, Miss Ellison, I don't know. The lawyer recommended the agency she's with, and when my cousin called, this is the agent they said had room in her schedule for handling an estate like ours."

"Mr. Hampton, if you can give me the name and contact information of the agent, I'd like to do some research to be sure she has experience in handling this kind of property. I have friends in real estate, and they're swamped right now, so her agency may be overwhelmed and forced to put her into the field. Don't sign a contract unless you are confident you have the right agent. Selling a condo near the beach is nothing like selling a historic site."

"Yes, ma'am, I'd appreciate that. It crossed my mind, but I haven't had time to check on it. And just call me Wallace."

She smiled. "Okay, Wallace. I like to be on a first name basis. I'm Mercedes, and this is Quincy."

Wallace nodded at Quincy. "Mercedes told me you're an archaeologist. You're welcome to poke around here, as long as you aren't alone. There are a lot of ways to get lost and hurt on the property. I have a guy who's worked around here for years, and if I can't be with you, he would be a great guide. Find some treasure so I can sell it and keep this place."

"I hope to do that if we can work it out. I have a flexible schedule."

"And I'm runnin' out of time to raise some money," Wallace said grimly. "Let's go look at the house, then I'll show you around the grounds."

Mercedes listened intently and made notes on her tablet as she and Quincy followed Wallace Hampton around. With a grand wave at the area to the front of the house, he pointed out that though there were two good roads to use as driveways, they should always use the second one they came to. The first led to a barn and public parking area for the landscaping nurseries and other services. "You followed my directions well today. Just remember to wait until you get to an avenue of old oaks, and it will be the private driveway to the front of the house. There's a path and you can get to the back porches from the other parking area, as well as the nurseries and cemetery. When the river was the main road, the back of the house was the front. They added this grand portico in 1790, in time for George Washington's tour of the Lowcountry, creating a new front entrance."

He led them through a tall flowering hedge along a flagstone and shell walk from the drive to the front portico of a Georgian-style mansion. Beside her, she heard Quincy catch his breath. Eight white, elegant columns stood as they had for over two centuries, impressive in their simple dignity. They were two stories high, three on each side of wide marble stairs and one on each end of the deep front portico. Arched brickwork created openings for basements and cellars in the raised foundation.

Wallace spoke like a tour guide accustomed to showing the property to visitors. "In the winter, these camellia japonicas will bloom in a riot of color, giving the mansion a festive air for the holidays. The only place around here with more varieties of camellias is Magnolia Gardens." He pointed in the direction where the other parking area must be if they could see it. "People come from all around to get some new bushes grown from ours in our nurseries when we have them. They get our oaks, flowering trees, and other landscaping plants."

Through gardens that led to the front of the mansion, Wallace showed them unusual botanical specimens and sunny, tropical shrubberies that grew well in the soil and climate. "These garden benches, freed people who chose to stay here made 'em. See that ironwork, with all the winding vines and leaves? There are no more made like this design around Charleston, even by Simmons."

Quincy's cellphone vibrated and he checked to see if it was urgent. It was.

"I'm sorry, this isn't a call I can ignore," he said. "You two go ahead, I'll catch up in a few minutes."

He stepped into the shade of a massive oak with an old bell suspended on an iron bar between two split trunks. He touched his phone screen to call the officer he contracted with for an antiquities fraud investigation that ended with the capture of the Lenoir Bassett and Madigan law firm. The investigation and arrests happened a month ago, and the officer said he had news about the case.

Other Books by Pamela Poole
<u>Southern Sky Publishing</u>[9]

The Painter Place Saga

Painter Place

Hugo

Jaguar

Landmark

3 Legend of Painter Place (short stories)

The Wind Songs of the Marsh

King's Ransom

The Castaway and the Mermaid

Southern Sky Devotional

Inspired Artistry—Embracing the Creative Calling

---

9. https://www.southernskypublishing.com/